Jack is prickly on his best days and an asshole on the worst ones. He loves that his brothers are finding their mates and have happy lives, but that's not for him. Who could stand to spend more than a few minutes with him apart from his family? Besides, he doesn't need anyone. He's not like his brothers, and he's fine on his own. Nothing and no one will change his mind about that.

Blair has a successful life, except for one thing — his love life. He's used to people taking advantage of him for gifts, money, or connections, and he doesn't expect anything different.

Until he meets his mate.

Jack and Blair are too different, and Jack knows it. He doesn't understand why Blair can't see it, no matter how hard he pushes Blair away. He also has trouble staying away, and when Blair invites him to a fundraising party, he can't say no.

Can two such very different people work together? Or, as Jack fears, are they destined to grow apart if they attempt to have a relationship?

As A Mule
Copyright © 2022 Catherine Lievens
ISBN: 978-1-4874-3576-9
Cover art by Angela Waters

Published by eXtasy Books Inc

Look for us online at:
www.eXtasybooks.com

As A Mule
Seven Brothers 6

By

Catherine Lievens

CHAPTER ONE

"Come on, we're going to be late," Andy yelled through Jack's door.

Jack grabbed his t-shirt from the bed and pulled it on as he opened the door. "I'm coming."

"About time," Andy muttered.

Jack rolled his eyes. "What's going to happen if we're late? It's not like Mom won't feed us."

"It doesn't mean we have to be rude."

Jack was tempted to roll his eyes again, but instead, he followed his brother to the front door of the apartment they shared. Andy had always been a stickler for being on time, while Jack believed that as long as he was only half an hour late, he was on time. It had always created some friction between them, but Jack wouldn't change his relationship with his brother for anything.

He couldn't say the same about his other brothers.

"Will Richie be there?" he asked as they took the elevator down. He patted his pockets to ensure he had everything he needed, thankful that Andy would be driving tonight. Considering most of the brothers would be there for the family dinner, Jack would need alcohol.

"I think so. Mom said something about Gilbert coming, and you know that where one of them goes, so does the other."

Jack huffed and followed Andy out of the elevator, then out of the building. "Why are they all finding their mates? It doesn't make sense that it's happening like this."

Andy looked amused. He'd listened to Jack rant about meeting—or rather, not wanting to meet—his mate many times since it had first happened to their brother Curtis. Only Jack and Andy were still single, and Jack knew Andy better than he knew any of his other brothers. Andy wanted to meet his mate, even though he wasn't saying it out loud.

"You can't tell me you're not happy Richie found his mate and that it's Gilbert."

"It could have been worse, I guess."

Andy laughed and unlocked the car. "Worse? Gilbert was part of our family even before he met Richie. This was the best outcome. Honestly, I'm not surprised he ended up being one of our mates."

Jack walked around the car and climbed in, glancing at Andy as he put on his seatbelt. "Did you want Gilbert to be *your* mate?"

Andy's cheeks flushed and kept his gaze firmly on the road, a sure sign Jack was right, at least in part. "Of course not. I already knew Gilbert wasn't my mate. I've known him longer than Richie, remember?"

"You had a crush on him at one point."

Andy groaned. "Can we not talk about that? I don't want to make things awkward for Gilbert and Richie, especially considering everything."

Jack tightened his hands into fists without even noticing it. He had to make a conscious effort to loosen them, but every time he thought about Richie and what had happened to him, he wanted to hit something.

He had to remember that Richie was safe. He'd left his ex behind, had met Gilbert, and had moved back. Gilbert and Richie shared a home now, and they were blissfully happy.

Jack still wanted to strangle Richie's ex with his bare hands.

"You're making that face again," Andy said.

"What face? This is the face I was born with."

"I'm pretty sure if you had been, Mom and Dad would have abandoned you at the hospital. You're looking quite murderous. I can't imagine how that would look on a baby."

Jack snorted. "Mom and Dad know me. They won't be surprised that I look murderous."

Andy was silent for a moment before gently asking, "Were you thinking about Richie?"

"What do you think I was thinking about? I should have killed the guy."

"But if you had, you'd be behind bars. It's good that you didn't, and besides, Richie is fine now. He's happy, and that's all that matters."

Jack agreed, just like he agreed that Richie looked happy.

Even though he was one of the youngest brothers, coming in after Hugh and Sean, Curtis, and Richie, and just before Andy and Laurie, he'd always felt protective of all his brothers. Curtis and Sean had never needed it. Hugh had always been awkward, but he was ten years older, and his twin had been there to protect him. On the other hand, Richie was only a few years older than Jack, so they'd been close, although not as much as Jack and Andy. Jack had felt the loss when Richie had moved away, but he'd thought his brother was happy.

Then he'd found out Richie had ended up with an abusive boyfriend.

Jack had a problem with anger. He got angry quickly, and once he had, it was hard not to hit something. Even thinking about what Richie had gone through made him want to hit something, possibly Richie's ex.

But the man was out of Richie's life. Richie had met his mate in Gilbert, and they were happy. They probably didn't even think about Richie's ex anymore, so why should Jack? The man was never coming back. He knew that if he tried anything, he'd have to deal with Richie's six brothers, plus a bunch of mates.

It would take a brave man to face all of them.

Jack was relieved and anxious when Andy parked in front of the house they'd grown up in. He spent a lot of time with his parents, but less so with his brothers, especially now that most of them were mated. It made Jack feel like he was the odd duck, or rather, the odd swan. The only other unmated brother was Andy, but Jack suspected that soon he'd lose his last brother to love, too. Andy was actively looking for his mate, even though it was like looking for a needle in a haystack. Jack, on the other hand, wasn't looking forward to it. Hell, some days, he hoped he *wouldn't* meet his mate. He didn't want to have to change his life to accommodate someone else, and he already knew that was what would happen if he met his mate.

"It looks like everyone's already here," Andy murmured as they left the car.

They had proof of that as soon as they opened the door and a wall of noise and people greeted them.

The house was big. It had to be. to accommodate seven brothers and their parents, but after the brothers had left, it had felt a bit empty when Jack visited. There was none of that emptiness tonight.

Like Andy had said, everyone was already there. As soon as Jack walked into the living room, he noticed his father sitting in his favorite armchair, Melissa in his arms. The baby was the daughter of Jack's youngest brother, which made him feel slightly inadequate. Laurie was barely twenty years old, yet he had a mate and a daughter. On the other hand, Jack was twenty-five, and he still shared an apartment with his brother.

The same went for everyone else. Richie and Gilbert had moved in together recently, and Curtis, Sean, and Hugh all lived with their mates. Curtis and Manuel were talking about having kids, and Jack's mother was over the moon. She wanted grandchildren, and Melissa wasn't enough for her, especially with seven kids. She didn't even care that all of them had male mates. Even Laurie, who'd always dated women, had found a male mate.

"There you are," Curtis said when he noticed Jack and Andy. "We were about to call you."

"We're not late," Jack protested.

"I beg to differ. We've been waiting for you to start eating, and I'm starving."

"You're always starving."

Shifters ate more than humans, because they needed the energy to shift back and forth. The meals had always been hefty, and now there was even more food packed on the huge dining table. The table had accommodated all seven brothers and their parents over the years, but now there were even more chairs around it, and when they sat down, Jack got Andy's elbow stuck in his ribs. He pushed his brother, and Andy pushed back, making Jack laugh.

"Look at the two of you," their mother said. "It's no wonder you haven't found your mates yet. You're like children."

Jack scowled. "I'm only twenty-five. Why would I want to meet my mate?"

Laurie loudly snorted. "Been there, done that. Fate won't care what you want or don't want. If it's time for you to meet your mate, you'll meet them."

"Maybe I'll run the other way," he muttered as he took the bowl of mashed potatoes and started filling his plate.

He'd always believed he'd be angry when he met his mate because he didn't want to have to change his life. But as he looked around the table, he wondered if maybe there was also something good about meeting your mate.

His brothers looked happier than they'd ever been, even Richie. He was at peace with Gilbert, and Jack watched them for a moment, finding them sickly cute as they fed each other bits of bread.

No, he was better on his own. If he met his mate, he doubted he'd be happy or that his mate would be. The man would probably take one look at him and run the other way, and Jack wouldn't stop him.

Blair tugged on his tie, breathing easier once it wasn't as tight around his neck. He peered into the empty offices as he walked past, but all of them were dark, a sure sign that he was one of the few left in the office. He wasn't the only one, though. When his sister had texted to ask if he wanted to have a late dinner with her and their father, he'd agreed. The three of them were still at work, and it wouldn't make sense for them to eat separately.

The door of their father's office was slightly open, and Blair knocked quickly before pushing. Their father was sitting behind his desk, while his sister was on the other side of it, curled into one of the chairs. She'd taken off her shoes, abandoning them on the carpet, and her feet were under her as she listened to whatever their father was saying.

He looked up when he heard Blair and smiled. "There you are. Dinner shouldn't be long."

"Good. I'm starving."

Lisa laughed. "Aren't you always starving?"

"I'm a growing boy."

"You're thirty-eight. If you grow, it'll be your stomach, not your height."

Blair was very much aware of that, which was one of the reasons he was careful about what he ate and tried to train every day. He always managed to find the time, although that wasn't hard, since he was single and had no children.

He flopped onto the other chair and stretched his legs out. "How are the kids?"

Lisa smiled. "They're great. Grant is still in his space period, and he's always spouting facts about planets and whatnot."

"You still think it's my fault?"

"You're the one who got him that space encyclopedia for his birthday."

"What else was I supposed to get him? He asked for it." Grant was eight years old, and he knew what he wanted. Blair had been more than happy to give him a book, since that was what he'd asked for, and he was glad to hear that Grant was still pleased with the gift.

"I know. I'm not complaining. At least he's learning stuff."

Her grimace told Blair who she was thinking about. "Natalie's still obsessed with video games?"

"I've tried everything, but the only thing that works is physically taking them away from her."

"I don't think video games are a bad thing."

Lisa shook her head. "They're not, but they can't be the only thing she does. She used to love reading, and now, she's always with that thing in her hands."

At least Blair hadn't been the one who bought the console for Natalie. Lisa only had herself to blame for that, and he knew she did.

These were the moments he was relieved he didn't have kids. He wouldn't have known what to do. On the one hand, video games weren't bad. On the other, it was true that Natalie spent many hours playing, probably too many. Lisa would have to find a way around that, and Blair wasn't looking forward to the fight she'd have on her hands.

There was a knock on the door, and the three of them turned to find their father's secretary standing there with bags in his hands.

"Dinner is here," Claude said.

Blair's father gestured at the long table he used for

meetings. "You can leave everything there and go home."

Claude dumped the bags onto the table, but he hovered there, not leaving even though Blair's father had told him to. "You're sure you don't need anything else from me?"

"No. You've done enough today. Go home."

"All right. I'll see you tomorrow morning."

"Have fun."

Claude softly snorted, which made Blair smile. His father and Claude had an odd relationship. In the beginning, when they hadn't known each other, they'd been quite rigid about their roles. Blair's father always had been when it came to personal assistants and secretaries, and Blair hadn't expected things to change. But his father had taken Claude under his wing, and sometimes, it felt as if Claude was like another son to him. Blair didn't mind. His parents only had two children, even though he knew they'd wanted more. If Claude made his father happy, then Blair was happy, too.

He, Lisa, and their father settled around the table. Lisa was still shoeless, and while Blair was tempted to do the same, he kept his shoes on his feet and his tie around his neck. He didn't want to have to put everything back on when he left, and there was no way he was running around the office without shoes on. Lisa could get away with it, but he couldn't.

"It's been a long day," Lisa said with a sigh as she grabbed one of the containers. She peeked inside, grinned, and snatched one of the forks from the table.

Their father had ordered Chinese, which Lisa loved. Blair didn't mind, but he made a mental note he'd have to train a bit longer tomorrow morning to make up for the calories.

"How come you're still here and not at home with your family?" Blair asked.

Lisa looked guilty. "I love them, but sometimes, they're even more tiring than the job."

Their father laughed. "I remember that from when you

were kids."

"But we're not anymore."

"Maybe so, but it doesn't mean your mother and I don't worry about you."

Blair tensed, knowing what was coming.

"Your mother asked me if she could set up a date for you for the party," his father said, staring at him.

Blair groaned. "Does she have to?"

"No, but you know how she is. She wants you to be happy."

"I *am* happy. Not everyone needs a relationship to be happy."

"We're aware of that, and I told her not to push, but you're almost forty. She'd like to see you settled before she dies."

Blair rolled his eyes. "She's sixty-four. She's not about to die."

"You could listen to what she has to say. One of her friends has a son she'd like you to meet."

Blair sighed and settled back in his chair. If he was honest, he wouldn't mind having a date for the party. Usually, he attended alone, which meant that at least a quarter of the people there tried to get their hands on him or sneak into the bathroom after him. It wasn't something Blair enjoyed, but he also didn't have time to build up a relationship.

He worked a lot. Everyone in their family did, including Lisa. No matter what she said about her kids being tiring, she missed them fiercely when she was at work. Sometimes, she wondered if she should have been a stay-at-home mom for longer than the few years she'd taken off the job. She and Blair talked about it often, but Blair didn't have any good insight. She loved her job, just like he did, and they were happy working for their father's real estate company, but Lisa's life was more complicated because she had a family.

Blair couldn't imagine dedicating himself to someone that

much. Besides, everyone he'd met and had a relationship with had used him for something. Usually, it was money, but sometimes, it was for jobs and connections. He didn't expect this meeting with his mother's friend's son to be any different. Everyone always wanted something from him, and right now, he wasn't willing to give anyone anything.

"I'll let her know," he said, knowing his father wouldn't just let this go.

His father sighed. "She worries about you. We both do."

"You shouldn't. I'm focused on the job, and in fact, I have a business trip in a few days."

"I'm aware of that. But you're not going far, are you?"

"I'll be back in time for the party."

The small town he was visiting was only an hour or so away by car. He was glad he'd be able to go in his own vehicle rather than taking a plane, and if he was honest, he was looking forward to having some time away from his family.

He loved them, but they could be pushy and nosy, even though they meant well.

Maybe they were nosy *because* they meant well. Whatever the reason, Blair was looking forward to having some time to himself.

Since Jack and Andy were the only ones alone tonight, they got roped into helping their mother clean up. Jack didn't mind. He was happy for his brothers, but did they *have* to be all lovey-dovey in front of him?

"You've been quiet tonight," his mother said as he handed her a stack of plates.

"Aren't I always quiet?"

"Not like that. And I saw you watching your brother."

"I was just making sure he was fine." Jack didn't have to ask which brother he'd been watching.

He'd kept an eye on Richie for most of the meal, trying to make sure Richie was fine. Not that Gilbert would hurt him, but what had happened with Richie's ex-boyfriend had been horrible, and Jack wouldn't be surprised if Richie still had nightmares and other stuff. But Richie had been smiling and laughing in a way Jack hadn't seen him do in a long time. Gilbert had been what Richie had needed, and even though Jack was grumpy about his brothers meeting their mates, he didn't resent them for it, and he was glad Richie had someone like Gilbert. Gilbert was a nice guy, and he was cute. Really, what could Richie want more?

"Your brother's fine," Jack's mother said. "Meeting Gilbert helped, and I'm glad he's home."

"I'm glad he's home, too." Jack turned to leave, but his mother wasn't done with him.

"I know Andy wants to meet his mate, too," she said.

Jack groaned. "Do we have to talk about this?"

"I suppose we don't have to, but I'm curious. Don't you want to meet your mate?"

Jack leaned back against the counter and crossed his arms over his chest. All his life, he'd watched his mother and his father. They were mates, and they were as much in love now as they had been when they'd met. Not that Jack had been there to see that, of course, but he'd seen enough pictures, and for as long as he could remember, they'd been the perfect couple.

They fought like every other couple, but they still stood strong after many years and seven children. One of the reasons was that they were mates.

"How much did you have to change when you met Dad?" he asked instead of answering her question.

Her smile told Jack she knew what he was talking about. His mother knew him well, but then, she knew all her sons well.

She rinsed the last plate and stacked it into the dishwasher before closing it and drying her hands. "Well, you always need to compromise when you meet someone you care about. The same goes when you meet your mate. Is that what you're worried about?"

Jack shrugged. "I like my life the way it is. I don't want to change because the guy I meet is perfect for me or whatever. Besides, who says he would be? No one's perfect."

"No one is," his mother agreed. "But I think that more than just being perfect, your mate will be perfect for *you*. It doesn't mean you won't fight or have to compromise, because that's what everyone needs to do when they're in a relationship. But whoever your mate is, he'll fit with you in a way no one else can." She paused and stepped closer, but thankfully, she didn't touch Jack. He wasn't a touchy-feely kind of person, even with his mother. "You've seen your brothers. Don't you want the same happiness?"

Jack didn't know how to answer that. In theory, he knew he should be happy if he met his mate. He hadn't yet, but the only thing he could think of was that when he did, he'd have to change.

He wouldn't be able to share an apartment with Andy anymore. There was no way his mate would want to live with Jack's brother. Jack was also grumpy on the best of days and insufferable when he was angry or annoyed. It was a miracle his family could deal with him, really, and he couldn't imagine someone would willingly stay by his side and go through that.

He'd had relationships, but none of them had lasted long. He hadn't wanted them to. He'd liked the guys he was with, but that was where things ended. It hadn't been love.

But it would be if he met his mate.

The thought annoyed him so much that he shook his head. His mother's eyes widened, and he realized what he'd just said no to.

"In theory, I do want to be happy," he said. "But I *am* happy now. I don't need someone in my life to be happy."

"Of course you don't. No one ever said you needed to have a mate or boyfriend. But you've always been the son I worry the most about."

That was news to Jack, who blinked. "I thought it was Laurie."

"Maybe I should have worried about him," Jack's mother said with a huff. "He became a father at twenty. Who in their right mind would do something like that, especially with no relationship and no job?"

"I'm sure many people want to be parents at twenty."

His mother's shoulders slumped. "And maybe it's the right thing for them, but Laurie wasn't ready."

"And you think that's why he met Alexis."

"I don't know. Maybe. But we're not talking about your brother now."

Jack gave his mother a crooked smile. "I thought I'd distracted you."

"Not so much that I don't remember what I was talking about." His mother sighed and came closer, gently touching his arm. "You've always been a protector. Even when it comes to Richie, who's older than you, you've always been there for him, ready to fight his battles. I tried to help you fight yours, but you wouldn't let me in, and that's what I want for you. I want you to have someone you can be yourself with. I want you to have someone you can trust and love with all of yourself and that you know they won't ever hurt you willingly. I want you to have someone to rely on the way your brothers rely on you."

Jack didn't know what to say. He could see his brothers were happy, and he was happy for them, but he'd always felt like he was on the outside looking in.

He was surprised his mother had noticed.

The twins had always had each other, and Curtis and Richie were close. Laurie had always done his own thing, but when it came to it, he and Andy were close, too. Jack and Andy lived together, and Andy was the brother Jack was closest to, but they were so different that sometimes Jack wondered if Andy could understand him.

Andy wanted what the other brothers had. He wanted love, a family, and a future with his mate. Laurie hadn't wanted to meet his mate, but in the end, when he had, he'd given in. Jack was glad he had, because Laurie had needed Alexis and they were perfect together, but he couldn't imagine himself doing the same.

Jack was fine the way he was, and he needed his mother to believe that.

He kissed her cheek and squeezed her in a quick hug. "I promise I'm fine. You don't have to worry about me."

"A mother always worries. I'll worry even when you're fifty."

Maybe that was why his mother wanted him to meet his mate. Maybe she wanted someone else to worry about him so she wouldn't have to.

"I promise you that I'm happy the way I am. Maybe I don't need a mate like my brothers."

Jack's mother's gaze was sad. "Everyone needs someone, even you. The fact that you do doesn't mean you're weak."

Jack didn't think that, but he believed that meeting his mate would create more problems than it would solve, which he wasn't looking forward to. Hopefully, his mate was far, far away, maybe on another continent, and Jack would never stumble on to him.

Lisa groaned as she slipped her feet back into her shoes. "Why do I wear heels again?" she asked.

She didn't expect an answer, but Blair teased her anyway. "I think you said they make your legs look longer."

"They're killing me," Lisa whined.

"Wear trainers tomorrow."

Lisa arched a brow and gave a pointed look at Blair's leather shoes. They weren't trainers, but they certainly weren't heels, either.

The elevator doors opened in front of them, and they stepped in. Lisa wobbled on her heels, and Blair reached out, offering her his arm. She took it with a smile and hugged it, leaning her head against Blair's shoulder as he punched the button to get them to the underground parking.

"How much longer do you think Dad will stay in his office?" Lisa asked.

"Not long if he knows what's good for him."

Lisa snickered. "Mom isn't going to be happy, although she liked that we had dinner together." Lisa paused and straightened. "And that Dad mentioned that thing about your date for the party."

Blair groaned. "Do we have to talk about this?"

"Not if you're opposed to it, but I'm worried, too."

"You do know that someone doesn't have to be married to be happy, right? I'm fine by myself."

"I know you are. I'm just worried you're too focused on work and that you forget how to live. When have you last taken a vacation?"

Blair frowned as he thought about it. He couldn't remember, which was probably a point in Lisa's favor. "So I'll take a vacation," he said.

She slapped his arm. "You know what I was trying to say. This doesn't have anything to do with vacations. You don't take time for yourself."

"The job is important."

"I suppose it depends. But I agree it's important to you and Dad."

"Not to you?"

She sighed heavily. "Sometimes, I wish I'd stayed at home with the kids."

"And the other times?" Lisa didn't need to work. Like Blair, she had a trust fund, and her husband was a famous lawyer. They had more than enough money for Lisa to have stayed at home until their kids were seventy. Instead, she'd decided to come back to work when Grant had turned three.

"The other times, I'm happy I came back. I need to work and feel like I'm doing something more than raising two kids. But I'm different. When I go home, my family is there. I spend time with Grant reading about space and bickering with Natalie about her video games. Then we play together for a while, and I put them to bed. I have something to look forward to at the end of every day, and someone to care for and who cares about me. Can you say the same?"

Blair thought about the empty apartment waiting for him. He liked having his own space and his privacy, but he couldn't deny that Lisa was right. He'd be happy to have someone to go home to, maybe someone to find asleep on the couch because they'd been waiting for him.

And he'd tried to get that, time and time again. He'd had relationships, and some of them had lasted a few years. Every time, though, things broke apart, to the point where Blair wondered if maybe there was something wrong with him. That thought was fleeting, but he couldn't help it when he saw how happy Lisa was with her husband and kids.

"When was the last time you had a relationship? Was it Kendra a few years ago?" Lisa asked.

"I'd rather not think about her." That had been a disaster, and Blair should have known better.

Lisa laughed. "I think we'd all rather not think about her. I don't think you were happy with her."

He hadn't been. Kendra was beautiful, and that had been the first thing Blair had noticed about her. He'd seen the signs that she was more interested in his wallet than in him, but he'd been lonely, and he'd ignored them. She'd started to push for a proposal after only being together for six months, and she'd planned to move into Blair's apartment without even talking to him about it. He'd put an end to it when he'd found out, and she'd been pissed, screaming that he didn't love her.

He didn't think he had. He certainly hadn't been about to propose, so they'd broken up. He hadn't cared that she'd gone around telling people he'd cheated on her and that he'd been bad to her. He didn't care what people thought, but it made it harder for him to find someone to be with in their social circle.

Maybe that was the problem. Maybe he needed to meet people who didn't know who he was or what he did. Not that doing so was easy when Blair spent most of his time working.

"Why don't you say yes to the date Mom wants to set you up on?" Lisa asked. "It doesn't mean you have to marry the guy. But you might have fun."

Blair couldn't think of anything less fun than being on a blind date during a fundraising party with people he worked with daily. "You're lucky you met Brian in college," he said.

As always when she spoke of her husband, Lisa's smile softened. "I was. I wish you'd been as lucky as I was."

The elevator doors opened, and Blair guided Lisa toward her car. "Not everyone can be as lucky as you and our parents." They'd also met their mates in college, and they'd been happy since then.

"You have to be open to a relationship if you want one," Lisa pointed out.

"I never said I wasn't open to a relationship. I've just gone through enough disasters to last me for a while."

"The date might not be a disaster."

Lisa opened her purse and dug for her keys. Since she wasn't looking at him, Blair rolled his eyes at her. She wouldn't let this go, and neither would their parents.

Blair didn't want a blind date, but he supposed he'd have to go along with it. If it reassured his family, maybe it wouldn't be a bad thing. "How about I'll agree to go on that date if I don't find anyone else to come with me?"

Lisa finally found her keys and snorted as she unlocked her car. "We both know it's easy for you to find dates. The problem is that you can't find love."

"I doubt I'll find love on a blind date."

"Fine, but you should tell Mom that."

"I will," Blair promised. Even if he couldn't find anyone to go with him, what would be the problem with a blind date? At the worst, it would be a disaster, and he'd never see the guy again. At least their first date would be in public with many people around. It should be easy enough to gently dump the guy once Blair decided he didn't want to be with him.

Lisa reached out and kissed Blair's cheek. "Go get some rest. You have that business trip in a few days, and then, the party."

"The business trip is only an hour or so away. I'll be fine."

"I know, but I feel guilty that you have to go on those trips for me."

Blair squeezed his sister in a tight hug. "I don't mind." And this way, she didn't have to leave her family behind.

Blair would gladly go on every business trip if it meant his sister could be with her family. Like she'd pointed out, it wasn't like he had anyone to go back home to anyway. The only thing waiting for him was his empty apartment, so he was kind of looking forward to the road trip, even though it would be only an hour long.

He'd known what he was signing up for when he'd talked to Lisa and their father about taking on most of the business trips, and he wasn't changing his mind.

He didn't have a reason to.

CHAPTER TWO

Jack was glad his workday was over. He liked working at the hardware store, but he ended up wanting to strangle at least one or two customers most days. That was probably why his brothers and his parents had been surprised when he'd decided to work there. Sometimes, he was surprised himself, and he wondered if there wasn't something better for him to do out there, but he enjoyed it. His boss, Mr. Thomas, had already told him that the store would be his once he retired. Neither of Mr. Thomas's sons wanted it, and neither of them even lived in town anymore.

Maybe that was why Jack continued to work there. Maybe he just wanted to be good to Mr. Thomas, and he disliked his sons, who'd abandoned their father.

Or maybe Jack was just weird.

Dealing with customers, and people in general, wasn't what he preferred, but he loved the smell of wood and metal that hung in the store. It was his second home, and while he wouldn't say he couldn't wait to go back tomorrow, it was a job he did happily.

He stopped at a red light and thrummed his fingers on his steering wheel. A light had lit up when he'd left the store's parking lot, and he knew it couldn't be good, but he also couldn't afford to stop at the moment. He'd go to the mechanic tomorrow, and hopefully, it wouldn't be anything bad.

The light turned green, and he accelerated. The real problems started when smoke appeared from the hood of the car. Jack's eyes widened, and he hesitated. Should he continue driving until he got home? Or risk the car exploding or something like that?

The car decided for him. It slowed down, even though he was accelerating, and the only thing he could do was guide it toward the side of the road. More smoke was coming out of the hood. As soon as the car stopped, Jack rushed out and opened it. He jerked back and closed his eyes when the smoke hit him in the face. He supposed he should be relieved the car wasn't on fire, but as he stared at the engine, he wasn't sure what to do.

He needed the car. He had to go to work, and he couldn't go on foot. He supposed he could ask Andy to give him rides, but that couldn't last forever. He also didn't have enough money to get a new car. He prayed this one would be easily fixed, but he had his doubts.

It wasn't the first time the car had problems, and the mechanic had warned him that eventually he wouldn't be able to fix it, not unless Jack wanted to sink too much money into it. They were at the point where fixing the old car would cost more than buying a used replacement, but Jack couldn't afford that, either.

There wasn't much he could afford, but he supposed that standing there in the middle of the road wouldn't help.

He leaned against the side of the car and took his phone out of his pocket. There were many people he could call. He had seven brothers, after all. He could also call any of their mates, and they'd come, too. But he didn't want to deal with his brothers, not even Andy. He was already anxious enough about the fact that he'd have to explain to Andy that his car had died and that he needed a ride to work tomorrow. Laurie was busy with Alexis and Melissa, Hugh disliked leaving his apartment on the best of days, and Sean was probably still at work.

Jack would call his father. He'd always told all of his

children to call him when they needed anything, even if it was a ride home after a party at three in the morning, but Jack had never taken advantage of it. He'd always found his way out of those situations on his own, but today, he didn't think he could.

He dialed the number and was about to hit the call button when a car stopped behind his. He turned his head to look at it, frowning when he saw it was a kind of car one didn't often see in a small town. It was too luxurious and cost too much, and it was out of place.

Just like the man who got out of the car was out of place.

The door opened, and the driver unfolded himself from the driver seat. Jack watched, pretty sure he was drooling, because the guy had to be the most handsome man he'd seen in a long time, if not ever.

As the man came closer, Jack noticed he was just a bit shorter than him, but not by much. He wore dress pants and a shirt, highlighting his broad shoulders and his narrow waist. His dark blond hair was swept away from his face and looked like it had been cut by someone who knew what they were doing. The man was wearing glasses, and it gave him an aura of a man who knew what he was doing.

It wasn't just the car that told Jack the guy was wealthy. Even though Jack never paid more than ten dollars for his clothes, he could tell that what the guy was wearing would be enough to pay his rent for a month, if not two. The shirt was stark white, the pants black, as were the leather shoes. The man was wearing a watch that looked as expensive as the car, and Jack briefly wondered why the man had stopped. Maybe he needed directions to go somewhere. He was not from here, and while he couldn't have missed the smoke coming out of Jack's car, maybe he thought it was a good idea to stop and ask Jack how to find wherever he was going.

"Good evening," the man said.

Jack even liked his voice—smooth, low, and it made Jack want to roll in it, even though it wasn't physically possible. "Hi," he croaked out, sounding and feeling like an idiot.

"I was looking for Clifton."

Jack frowned. "The town?"

"Yes. Can you tell me where it is?"

Jack gestured. "You're in it."

The man blinked and looked around.

Jack would be the first to admit Clifton wasn't much. It was a small town, which was what his parents had been looking for when they'd decided to settle down here. They'd wanted to raise their children in a small community, and they'd managed.

The town wasn't tiny, but it wasn't huge, either. Most of the stores were on Main Street, and those that weren't were big box stores that were convenient but didn't have the same charm.

"If you go back, you'll hit Main Street. Whatever you're looking for, you'll probably find it there."

"I researched the town, but I didn't realize it was so small," the man said, still looking around.

"Yes, well, it is. Welcome to Clifton, I guess."

Jack had better things to do than to worry about a lost tourist, so he turned back to his car. He still hadn't called his father, and he didn't fancy spending the night on the side of the road. With his luck, one of his brothers would drive by and see him.

"Is everything okay?" the man asked, stepping closer.

"Does it look like everything is okay?" Jack snapped.

"No. It looks like you need some help."

"I'll get help. I was just calling someone. You don't have to stick around. Clifton is small, and there's hardly any crime. No one will try to rob me or anything."

"That's not what I was worried about."

Dammit. The man's voice made Jack want to step closer and bury himself into the man's arms so he could forget about his problems, car included.

Jack cleared his throat. "What were you worried about then?"

"It's getting dark, and you're standing on the side of the road. What happens if a car doesn't see you?"

Well, that wasn't smart, but he'd never admit that to a stranger. "I'll just get back in my car. Don't worry about me."

He moved to do just that, but the man came even closer. The wind turned, pushing away the smell of smoke, and Jack was hit with a new scent, one that could only come from the man standing close to him.

Jack's back went ramrod straight.

It couldn't be. There was just no way.

This man couldn't be his mate.

For some reason, the pretty man jerked back when Blair came closer. It took Blair a moment to realize that he was probably freaked out by a stranger trying to go near him, so he raised his hands to show the man he wasn't a danger. "My name is Blair," he said.

The guy still looked like he'd seen a ghost. He was holding his phone so hard that Blair wouldn't have been surprised if it had cracked.

"I'm not trying to hurt you. I'm just worried about you," Blair continued.

The man shook his head. "I'll be fine. You should go."

But Blair had no intention of abandoning the man here. He didn't know what it was, but he felt protective of this man. He wanted to make sure nothing happened to him, and if there was anything he could do, he'd do it.

He stepped even closer, and there was nowhere for the

man to go. He pressed his back against his car. His eyes were wide, and he was gaping while also looking like he didn't know where to look.

Was Blair so intimidating? He didn't usually have this problem, not even at work. He didn't understand what was happening.

He offered the man his hand. "I'm Blair," he repeated.

The man stared at Blair's hand as if it were a snake. Blair waited. The wind picked up, and the smell of smoke hit Blair in the face. He wrinkled his nose, then froze at the scent underneath the smoke.

It wasn't anything he'd smelled before, yet somehow, he recognized it, and he knew who it belonged to. He hadn't expected something like this to happen out here, on an empty road in a small town he hadn't even realized he was in. He'd thought that when and if he met his mate, it would be someone who belonged to his social circle, someone who would fit in his life without having to try. He'd been wrong, and he still didn't know his mate's name. But this had to be why his mate looked so spooked. He hadn't expected to meet Blair, but then, no one ever expected to meet their mate.

But what if Blair's mate wasn't feeling well? Maybe that was why he was so scared. Blair wanted to do something, but he didn't know what. "Are you feeling all right?" he asked.

His mate glared at him. "Of course."

"Because it doesn't look like it. You haven't even told me your name."

"I'm Jack."

Blair had a name.

And he had a date for the party.

The thought made him smile.

"Why are you smiling?" Jack snapped.

"Because I met you. Isn't meeting your mate the best day of your life?"

Jack crossed his arms over his chest. "I wouldn't know about that. It's probably a mistake, anyway."

Blair shook his head and leaned closer. Jack squawked, but there was nowhere for him to go, and so close, Blair could smell him even better.

Jack was his mate. There was no denying that.

"Why are you here on the side of the road?" he asked.

Jack gestured at his car. "Why do you think? It broke down while I was driving home."

"Have you already called someone for help?"

"No. I was about to when you stopped."

"I'll give you a ride home."

Jack snorted. "And you think I'm going to climb into a car with someone I don't know? You could be a serial killer, for all I know."

Blair supposed it made sense, except for one detail. "I'm not a serial killer. I'm your mate."

"And? It doesn't mean you're not a serial killer. Besides, how can we be sure we're mates?"

"You smell it, too. You can't deny what we are."

Jack's glare was so fierce that Blair wouldn't be surprised if that was what had set fire to his car. "The only thing I know is that you smell good."

"I recognize you as my mate. My Osprey recognizes you." Which made Blair wonder what kind of shifter Jack was. He sniffed discreetly, but the only thing he got was the scent of shifter and smoke.

"You're an Osprey shifter?" Jack asked.

"I am." Blair hoped Jack wasn't a prey shifter because it would freak him out even more. Not that Blair would hurt him in any way. He was a shifter, not an animal, and even though his Osprey was telling him to grab Jack and pull him into his arms, it wasn't to eat him.

At least not in the food kind of way.

Jack nodded as if what Blair had said made sense. He didn't tell Blair what kind of shifter he was, though, so Blair asked, "What kind of shifter are you?"

Jack stared for so long that Blair thought he wouldn't answer. Eventually, though, he shrugged and said, "I'm a swan shifter."

Blair liked swans. They were elegant and beautiful but also fierce. Jack sounded like he'd fit right in Blair's life.

"Well, let me give you a ride home," Blair said again. "I promise I'm not a serial killer. I won't hurt you. I just want to make sure you're safe." And possibly get Jack's phone number.

He was hoping that during the ride, Jack would relax. He understood being shocked. He was, too. The last thing he'd expected when he'd gone on this business trip was to meet his mate. He'd expected to be in and out of the small town in a few days, then to go on that blind date his mother wanted to organize for him. Instead, he'd met Jack, and even though they'd known each other for only a few minutes, the man already meant everything to him.

Blair would do everything he could to make Jack happy, and as he eyed the car still smoking behind his mate, he knew what his first gift would be.

"I already told you I could do this on my own," Jack said.

Blair's mate was stubborn, but that was okay. Blair's parents always said he had the patience of a saint, and he would need it with Jack.

"But you don't have to do it on your own. I'm here, and I have a car. It's fine if you'd rather bother your family or your friends to come to get you, but there's no need. I'm right here, and I think we need to talk." Even Jack wouldn't be able to deny that. They were mates, and they had to talk about it, even if it was only to reject each other.

Blair hoped that wouldn't happen. He had no intention of

rejecting Jack, and he hoped Jack would give him a chance before doing so. He looked angry and tired, which probably was why he was keeping his distance. It was evening, so he'd probably just left work, and his car had died on him. That would be enough to ruin anyone's day and make meeting your mate more of a problem than something to celebrate.

Blair didn't want to push Jack into doing something he wasn't ready for. But it felt like if he let Jack call one of these family members, he'd never see his mate again. He didn't even have Jack's phone number, and even if Jack didn't want to talk to him right now, they needed something to link them.

"I don't want to force you to accept a ride from me," he said slowly. "It's fine if you want to call your family. Can you please give me your phone number, though?"

For some reason, that made Jack shake his head. "You don't need my phone number."

"I'm your mate. I want to be able to call you."

Jack rubbed his face. He looked tired, which made Blair want to take care of him. He wanted to pack up Jack, get him some food and a bed, possibly with him in it, too. Instead, they were stuck on the side of the road until Jack gave in.

Blair was going to have his hands full with Jack. He didn't mind. If Jack agreed to be in his life at all, he'd view it as a blessing. He didn't care how stubborn Jack was. He could deal with it. He dealt with a lot of things and clients who pushed his patience to the edge. He'd be happy to have Jack do it since, hopefully, he was in his life to stay.

Jack wanted to tell Blair to fuck off and leave, but something stopped him. He wasn't sure what it was. He didn't want a mate, and he had no intention of giving Blair the time of day.

But Blair looked like if Jack said no, he'd find a way to contact him anyway. He had that stubborn expression Jack recognized so well because he got it, too, almost daily. Blair wouldn't let this go, and the only thing Jack could do was go along with it.

Besides, what could it hurt to give Blair his phone number? Blair might call him, but Jack didn't have to answer. He still didn't know if he'd want to, and he wasn't going to find out now. He just wanted to go home and forget about all of this.

But he couldn't go home. There was no way he was giving Blair his address. He didn't know the man, but he seemed used to getting what he wanted. Jack suspected that if he gave Blair his address, he'd find his mate at his doorstep whether he liked it or not.

But Blair expected him to say yes to the ride and tell him where to go.

Jack looked down at the phone he was still holding. It would be easier to call his father, but Jack suspected Blair would still be around when his dad arrived. Then Jack would have to explain who Blair was to his father, which meant the entire family would know about it in half an hour. He couldn't deal with that or with his brothers. So even though there was nothing he wanted less, he nodded curtly.

"You can give me a ride," he said.

For some reason, that seemed to delight Blair. "Good. Will you also give me your phone number?"

"Will you stop asking if I say no?"

"No. I've been known to wear people down until they give me what I want."

"Of course you have," Jack muttered.

He opened his car and leaned in to grab his wallet and house keys. He slid the car key out of the slot, closed the door, and locked the car. He gave the engine one last glance, made sure everything was secure, and followed Blair to his car. He was going to have to call the mechanic, and soon. He couldn't leave the car abandoned out here, and it wasn't like he could drive it away. He cringed when he thought about how much this would cost him.

But his mate didn't seem to have problems when it came to money. The car he drove was sleek and looked like it cost a lot. Jack wasn't one for cars, but even he could tell. The car was a dark gray and gleamed under the streetlamps. A small B with wings on both sides stood out in front, and he was sure that if he'd been a car guy, he would have recognized at least the maker. Instead, he shrugged and slid into the passenger seat.

He looked around as Blair got situated in the driver's seat. The seats were white leather, and the inside of the car was a mix of dark blue and white. Blair looked at home there, and he quickly drove him away from Jack's car.

"You have to give me an address," he said.

"I'll tell you where to go."

"I have a GPS. We can use that."

Jack peered at the complicated-looking screen. "You don't need it. I've lived here all my life, and I know where we're going." There was no need for Jack to enter his parents' address so Blair could use it to find him.

Blair didn't seem angry at Jack's refusal but rather amused. Jack had the impression that Blair had been amused the entire time they'd been together. He didn't understand it, which made him angry, but he knew better than to snap. His brothers and parents knew how he was, but Blair didn't. Jack might have no intention of ever calling the man, but he still didn't want to mistreat his mate.

"So, you were headed home when your car died," Blair said as he drove.

"How do you know that?"

"An educated guess. Isn't that where you were going?"

Jack huffed. "Yeah, I was going home."

"What do you do? Where were you coming from?"

"From work. I work at the hardware store here in town." Jack held his breath, wondering what Blair would think of that. Obviously, whatever Blair did for a living, he earned a lot of money. Everything about him screamed wealthy, which was so far from Jack that it wasn't even funny.

But Blair didn't seem to have a problem with Jack's job. He nodded, then asked, "I'm afraid I don't know much about hardware stores. Can you tell me what you do?"

Jack couldn't tell what Blair was thinking, but he didn't sound derisive. "I take care of customers and refill the shelves, go over the inventory, things like that. I know it's not much considering how old I am, but I like the job."

"Well, I don't know if I'd say it's not much. And I don't think it depends on your age. How old are you? You seem young."

But Blair didn't. Jack hadn't been able to see much while they'd been standing by his car, but he'd given Blair a good look when they'd climbed into the car with the light on. He was as gorgeous as he'd been in the darkness, but Jack had been able to see slight signs of age, like the tiny lines around Blair's eyes. Two deeper ones creased the space between Blair's eyebrows, and Jack wondered if it was because he frowned too much. Blair wasn't old, but he also wasn't as young as Jack.

"I'm twenty-five," Jack said.

Blair took it like he had when Jack explained about his job—with a nod and a smile. "Quite a bit younger than me, then."

"How old are you?" Jack didn't want to know anything about Blair, yet at the same time, he wanted to know everything. That was his human side and his shifter side fighting. The swan wanted nothing more than to cuddle into Blair's arms, but Jack couldn't afford for that to happen.

"I'm thirty-eight."

It was older than Jack had expected. "That's thirteen years."

"It is. Am I too old for you?"

"I didn't say that."

"I'm relieved. I wouldn't want you to think I'm too old for you."

Jack looked out the window and rolled his eyes. He told Blair to turn right, then left, then he asked the question he'd wanted to ask. "What do *you* do for a living?"

"I work for my father."

"That doesn't tell me anything."

Blair chuckled. "I suppose it doesn't. My father owns a real estate business. Both my sister and I work for him."

Somehow, Jack doubted it was the same as the real estate agency in town. He didn't know how all of that worked, but he could imagine Blair buying skyscrapers or things like that. "That sounds boring."

Blair laughed. Jack had been trying to offend him, but he was starting to understand it would take a lot for that to happen. Jack hadn't expected it, but Blair seemed easy-going, much more than he was.

"I suppose it can be," Blair said. "It depends on what you're interested in. My sister and I grew up with our father building the business, so we were immersed in it from a young age. I doubt I'd be happy working in a hardware store like you do."

Jack was sure of that. He couldn't even imagine Blair *in* the hardware store.

He didn't know what to do. Blair was his mate, and Jack was aware that if he rejected him, he wouldn't get a second one. He didn't *want* one, either. He didn't know what to do with the first, let alone a second.

But could he reject Blair? Wasn't he supposed to give him at least a chance? His family would be disappointed if he didn't, but they had no say in this situation. The only ones who did were Jack and Blair.

"You accepted the fact that we're mates easily," he said. He wanted to understand and find out if there was a way to make this easier.

Blair quickly looked at him before turning his attention back on the road. "Haven't you?"

Jack almost laughed. There was nothing easy in this situation, but he wasn't sure Blair understood that.

Something was going on, and Blair didn't understand what. He wanted to ask Jack, but he was starting to realize that Jack was contrary. He seemed to enjoy doing the opposite of what Blair expected him to do, which left Blair not knowing what to do next.

Jack shrugged and looked out the window. "I don't like the fact that someone out there decided we were perfect for each other when we didn't even know each other."

"I don't think that's how it works. I know the stories about fate and all of that, but I suspect it's a biological thing. Your shifter side and mine recognized each other, and we feel drawn."

"Wouldn't that be the case with many people, though? Instead, we only have one mate."

"And I'm glad that mate is you."

Jack seemed nonplussed by Blair's words. "How can you say something like that?"

"Why shouldn't I? You're my mate, and I only have one of you. That means I'll do anything I can to make you happy."

"Don't you want to fight it?"

Blair frowned. Was that what Jack had been doing since they'd met? Fighting his attraction to Blair? At least now, some of his behavior made sense. "Why should I fight it?

However it's decided, whether because of fate or biology, there's no denying that you're my mate and that you're perfect for me. We can't ignore the bond that pulls us together."

"Turn here," Jack snapped.

"Is that what you want to do?" Blair asked as he obeyed. "You want to fight the bond?"

"I don't know what I want," Jack said. He sounded angry but also lost. "I don't even know you."

"And I don't know you, but while you don't seem to want to get to know me, I do want to get to know you. I'd like for you to give me a chance to show you I'm not a bad person."

"I never said you were a bad person. There, park in front of that house, the one with the red flowers."

Blair obeyed and turned the car off. Jack looked conflicted, and while Blair wanted to help, he didn't know how or even if he could.

He did understand where Jack was coming from. Some people had trouble accepting their mate because they felt like the decision of who to be with had been taken out of their hands. Blair didn't see things that way, though. He also saw no good reason to fight the bond. Jack was his mate, and that was that. Now, they needed to learn to be together.

The curtain in one of the windows moved, and a woman's face appeared. Blair blinked, wondering who she was. Did Jack still live with his parents? Or did he have a girlfriend? Blair should probably have asked earlier, but he hadn't thought about it.

"Do you have a girlfriend?"

Jack looked taken aback. "Gosh, no. Why do you ask?"

"Because a woman is staring at us from the window."

Jack groaned. "That's my mother."

"So you live with your parents?"

Jack twisted in his seat to look at Blair. "No. I have an apartment. I just didn't want you to know the address."

Blair was a little hurt, but he understood. "In case I'm a serial killer?"

That caused Jack to bark out a laugh. "Exactly. So I gave you my parents' address. This is the house I grew up in."

It was pretty. Someone cared a lot about the house and the yard in front of it. Blair could easily imagine Jack growing up here and the two of them visiting often.

Jack's eyes narrowed. "I'm close to my family, including my six brothers. In fact, I live with one of them."

He seemed to expect Blair to have a problem with that for some reason. Blair didn't, although he was stunned that Jack had six brothers. "I'm close to my sister, too. My parents wanted more children, but my mother couldn't, so it's only the two of us. Seven sounds like a handful."

Jack's expression relaxed. "If you ask my mother, she'll tell you all about it." He seemed to realize what he'd said, and his expression shuttered again. "I need to go."

"You said you'd give me your phone number," Blair said before Jack could disappear into the night.

"I never said I would. You asked for it, and I wanted to know why, but I never said I would give it to you."

Blair needed that phone number. How else would he find his mate? He supposed he could come back here, but he doubted Jack's parents would be happy to find him on their doorstep.

But Jack didn't want to give Blair his phone number. Blair didn't understand what he was afraid of, but he didn't have to. These were Jack's fears, and they were legitimate. Pushing wouldn't help, and Blair didn't want to hurt Jack.

"How about I give you my phone number?" he suggested, leaning closer but keeping enough distance between them so that Jack wouldn't feel boxed in.

"You want to give me your number?" Jack sounded surprised.

"Yes. That way, you can call me whenever you want. I'll always answer."

"Even in the middle of the night?"

"Even if you call me at three in the morning," Blair promised.

"Even if you're in the middle of an important business meeting?"

It was clear Jack wanted to know that Blair would put him first, and Blair was more than happy to do just that. "Even if I'm in a business meeting with the Pope."

That brought a smile to Jack's lips.

Blair liked it, and he liked the fact that he'd been the one to put it there even more.

"If that ever happens, you should probably talk to the Pope. But fine. Give me your number."

Blair quickly took a business card out of his wallet. It had his office number and his business cell, so he quickly added his personal cell number to the back. "Call me anytime on this number. I'll always answer."

Jack stared at the business card for a moment before taking it. "This is crazy," he murmured.

"It might be, but we'll make sense of it." As long as they worked together—but Blair wasn't a hundred percent sure they would. It all depended on Jack now.

Blair could show Jack he'd be there for him and that he cared about him. Maybe that was what Jack needed. He was afraid to give in, which meant he was scared to trust Blair. Blair would have to show him he cared and was in this for the long run.

"I need to go," Jack said. He clutched the business card and opened the passenger door. "If I don't, my mom is going to come out and start asking questions, and you don't want that to happen."

"I'd be delighted to meet your mother."

Jack snorted. "Say that again after you meet her. She'll try to mother you, even though you have your own mother."

"I do." And it sounded like the two mothers would get along splendidly once they met.

Blair couldn't wait for that to happen.

Jack gave him an awkward little wave and slammed the door shut. He didn't look back. But Blair stayed where he was, and he watched his mate rush to the front door and throw it open. He disappeared inside, and the curtain at the window lowered.

Blair smiled. He could imagine the conversation Jack and his mother were having, and he was glad he'd driven Jack home. This way, at least someone would know about Blair, which meant Jack wouldn't be able to ignore the entire situation like Blair had no doubt he'd been planning on doing.

For some reason, Jack was reticent about having a mate. Luckily, Blair was patient and crafty. He'd find a way around Jack's fears, and if he couldn't, well, he'd do everything he could so that Jack could get rid of them.

He waited a few more seconds. Then he turned the car on. He had things to do, and the sooner he got started on them, the better it would be for Jack.

CHAPTER THREE

"It's dead."

Jack groaned. He'd expected that answer from the mechanic, but he'd hoped that against all odds, his car would make it. "You can't fix it?"

"I could, but honestly, it wouldn't be worth it."

"Are you sure?"

The mechanic shook his head. "You'd have to sink a few thousand dollars into it, at least. Besides, that's not the only problem I found."

Jack's father squeezed Jack's shoulder. "Let it go," he murmured.

Jack knew his father was right, but how was he supposed to do that? He couldn't be without a car. He needed to go to work at the very least. "Fine. Let it die then," he said.

There was some paperwork after that, but Jack was pouting. This was a disaster, and he wasn't sure how to get out of it.

His father stayed silent until they left the mechanic shop and climbed into his car. Only then did he offer, "Your mother and I could help."

"I don't need you to."

His father looked like he didn't believe him, and he wasn't wrong. Jack did need help, but he didn't want to ask his parents.

He wasn't sure why. He wouldn't be the first of his brothers that their parents helped. When Curtis had moved back home, he'd stayed with them and had worked with their father. Laurie needed help seemingly every week, mostly with childcare but also with child-related stuff. Richie, too, had needed help when he'd come back, and everyone had been more than happy to give him a hand.

But Jack felt like he shouldn't need anyone, least of all his parents. He was an adult. He should be able to get himself a new car because his old one had died or to get himself an apartment he didn't have to share with his brother.

Money wasn't the only reason he and Andy shared a place, though. Jack had always lived with a bunch of other people, and even going from being at home with eight other people to only living with Andy had been strange. Jack could only imagine how weird it would be to be on his own, and it had nothing to do with rent.

Jack's father sighed. "You've always been the most independent of our sons, and I don't know why. Did we do something?"

"Of course not. You and Mom are great. But I'm twenty-five, and I shouldn't need your help."

"Do you feel the same about Richie? Or Curtis? When they came home, they both needed our help, and we were happy to do anything we could for them. How are you any different?"

That was what Jack had just been thinking, and he wasn't surprised his father had read him so well.

Of his parents, his mother was the chatty one. She always checked on her sons, ensuring they were okay and asking about their days. Jack's father was quiet, maybe too much so, but he was always there when they needed him. He'd offered Jack a ride to the mechanic after work without Jack having to ask. Now, it sounded like he was offering to help Jack get a new car. Jack desperately wanted to say yes because it would be a huge problem that wasn't on his shoulders anymore, but he couldn't find it in himself to do so.

"I'm not different. But Richie's situation was what it was, and no one blamed him for needing help."

"What about Curtis, then?"

"He'd just broken up with his boyfriend when he came back. He needed to be with family."

"But you don't? It's just a car, Jack, and your mother and I can afford it."

Jack might have to say yes. "I'll let you know," he said instead because he didn't want to say something he'd regret.

He was relieved when they reached his parents' home. He enjoyed spending time with his father, but he needed some time alone to pout and mope after what happened with his car. Once that was over, he'd be able to focus on how to get a car. Unfortunately for him, he wasn't the only one of his brothers who enjoyed spending time at his parents' home. When he got there, he noticed Leon's car right away. Laurie was there, too, no doubt with Melissa and probably Alexis, because those two were never far from each other.

This wasn't going to be pleasant.

Jack was tempted to stay in the car, but he didn't want to look like an idiot, so he climbed out and followed his father to the front door. The wall of noise that greeted him when they walked in was familiar, and it soothed something inside of him. Whatever happened, whatever he needed, he'd always have his family. Even though he didn't want to ask for help, they'd be there for him when he didn't have another choice.

He realized how lucky he was to have such a safety net. It wasn't only his parents, either. His brothers would do anything they could for him if he asked, something he seldom did. He didn't want to owe anyone, least of all the people who teased him endlessly.

But then, he did the same to them.

He found his mother in the kitchen, bouncing Melissa on

her knee while Laurie was sipping on coffee. Leon was cooing at the baby, and Alexis was at the stove, cooking something. That was a surprise, because Jack's mother didn't usually enjoy having other people cook in her kitchen, but she was busy with Melissa, which made sense. The little girl was her favorite person in the world, possibly even more so than Jack's father.

Every single one of them turned to look at him when they heard him.

He hadn't told anyone about Blair, not even his mother. She'd been the one watching them yesterday evening, but when she'd asked what happened, he'd explained his car had broken down and that a stranger had stopped and given him a ride before he could call anyone. She hadn't been happy about the fact that he'd accepted a ride from a stranger, and she'd asked why Jack had spent so much time in the car once it was parked in front of the house, but luckily, Jack had managed to avoid answering. Melissa had been there, too, and his mother had been otherwise occupied.

So no one knew about Blair. No one would be asking questions about him, which was what Jack wanted. He still didn't know what he wanted to do about his mate, and he hadn't called Blair yet. He hoped that waiting for a while would help him make a decision, but so far, he was torn.

His shifter side wanted him to call Blair and give him anything he wanted because he was his mate. However, Jack's human side still disliked the fact that someone somewhere had decided Blair was the perfect man for him. He wasn't sure that was correct, anyway. He and Blair were so different that he didn't feel they could work together, let alone be mates.

There was no denying how Blair had smelled yesterday, even though Jack wondered if it had been a mistake. It could have been if he'd been the only one to realize Blair was his mate, but Blair had smelled the same, so it couldn't be.

He was tempted to leave the kitchen so he wouldn't have to deal with his brothers, but instead, he sat at the table and snatched Laurie's cup of coffee. Laurie made a protesting sound, but Jack was already sipping. He grimaced and pushed the mug back toward his brother. "There's so much sugar in this that you could stand a spoon up in it," he complained.

"Maybe you should get your own coffee, then," Laurie said with snark.

"How are you able to sleep when you drink this stuff at night?"

Laurie didn't get to answer because someone rang the doorbell. They looked at each other. The only ones who visited regularly were the brothers, and they didn't ring the bell. Their mother would kick their ass if they tried. Even though they didn't live here anymore, she insisted it was still their home, so they didn't need to knock.

"It's probably a delivery," Laurie said. "Mom, did you order something?"

She shook her head and started handing over Melissa, but Jack got to his feet before she could. "I'll go," he said.

She gave him a grateful smile. "I'm not expecting anything, so it shouldn't be important."

Jack nodded and headed to the front door. His father was opening the door as he got there, though, so he stopped and started turning around to go back to the kitchen.

"Jack?" his father called out.

"What is it?"

"This gentleman says he has something for you."

Jack swallowed, his knees suddenly weak. Was it Blair? The word gentleman would describe him to a *T*, but Jack prayed his mate hadn't decided to come to meet his parents.

His hands shook as he walked toward his father and peeked outside. He was relieved when he saw Blair wasn't standing on the doorstep, but that only lasted for a few moments because he saw the car parked in front of the house.

The man standing on the doorstep held out his hand, and Jack numbly took what he was holding out.

Car keys.

"All the documents are in the car," the man said. "Have a good evening."

Jack watched him turn around and walk away. His father didn't say anything right away, but Jack could feel his gaze on him.

How the fuck was he going to explain this to his family?

Blair was wrapping up the meeting when his phone vibrated on the table. It was rude to leave it there, but he hadn't wanted to miss any phone calls in case Jack decided to contact him. He'd suspected Jack would do so after the car was delivered, and he'd been looking forward to it.

He snatched the phone and looked up. "It was a pleasure doing business with you," he told the people around the table. "If you need anything, call my secretary, and she'll make sure to solve any problem you might have or put you in contact with me."

The people around the table nodded their goodbyes, and Blair got to his feet. He was answering the phone before he left the room.

"Hello?"

"What the fuck did you do?"

Blair was right. It *was* Jack, and he sounded angry, which wasn't surprising, either. "Good evening to you too, Jack. How are you?"

"Stop that. I'm pissed. You had no right to buy me a car."

"I'm your mate."

"That doesn't mean you can buy me a car! How much did

you even pay for it? It looks more expensive than my entire apartment."

"What does it matter? I can afford it. You won't have to pay anything. I've already insured it, so the only thing you have to do is drive it."

"I found the documents. I know it's insured. But I can't accept this."

Jack did sound angry, but Blair didn't understand. He wasn't surprised that was the case, but he wished Jack would explain what was going on.

He left the building, needing to be alone. He didn't want anyone to overhear this conversation. "Why can't you? You're my mate. It makes sense that I would buy you gifts and things you need."

"But not a car."

"Don't you like it? I can get you another one if you'd rather pick something different."

"That's not what I was talking about. You really don't understand, do you?"

"No. I don't."

There was a moment of silence, and Blair wondered if Jack was going to hang up on him. He wouldn't be surprised if Jack tried to find a way to give him the car back, but Blair had already decided he wouldn't take it. If Jack wanted something different, he'd be more than happy to give it to him, but he wasn't taking the car back just because Jack felt it wasn't right for Blair to buy it for him.

"Come to the house," Jack ordered.

Blair blinked. He hadn't expected that. "Really?"

"We can't do this on the phone. I want to strangle you, and for that, I need to get my hands on you."

"I'd rather have you get your hands on me for something different."

Jack spluttered. "Just come. I want to yell at you in your

face."

He hung up, leaving Blair to stare at the screen until it turned dark.

Was Jack going to yell at him? From what little Blair knew about his mate, it was possible. Jack seemed prickly, and he wouldn't have called if Blair hadn't bought him a car.

Blair didn't understand why Jack had so much trouble accepting they were mates. There was no denying it, and the fact that they were mates meant they were destined to be together. Yet, Jack hadn't seemed happy about that, and he was fighting the bond. Why? Was Blair so far from what Jack had expected and wanted from a mate? Maybe that was the problem. Blair hadn't thought about it before because just like Jack was perfect for him, he was supposed to be perfect for Jack, but maybe something had gone wrong. Maybe Jack didn't like the way he looked or his personality.

Not that he knew a lot about Blair. They'd barely talked yesterday. Still, it was a possibility Blair had to keep in mind, no matter how little he liked it.

He'd know more after talking to Jack, so he climbed into his car and started it. He remembered where the house was, but he still entered to address in his GPS. He didn't want to be late because he'd got lost.

He had no idea what he'd find when he reached the house, except for the car and Jack. Jack's parents were probably there, too, and that might be another reason Jack was angry. From what Blair had gathered, he wasn't planning on telling his parents he'd met his mate. Blair hadn't meant to force his hand, but he hadn't known where else to have the car delivered. He'd hesitated between Jack's parents' house and the hardware store, but he'd thought the store would be even worse.

Several cars were parked in front and the driveway when he reached the house. That had been the case yesterday, too.

And it was clear there were more people than just Jack's parents in the house. Blair didn't have to wonder if he was about to meet everyone. Before he could even get out of his car, the front door flew open, and Jack stomped out.

He was angry. It gave Blair pause, but no matter how many times Blair asked himself if buying a car for his mate was a bad thing, he didn't understand how Jack thought.

He stepped out of the car, eager to get this over with. Whatever was about to happen, Blair knew he'd be able to convince Jack to accept the car. He was used to dealing with people as prickly as Jack, and he was confident in his abilities.

"Jack?" a woman asked from the doorstep.

Jack paused before he could reach Blair. "What is it?"

"Can you tell us what's going on? We're worried."

"And we want to know about your car," a man said.

Jack wasn't the only one who'd left the house. Little by little, people started coming out and lining the porch. There was an older woman and a man, probably Jack's parents. A very young man stood next to Jack's mother, holding a baby and looking delighted by everything happening. Another young man stood next to him, hovering close by as if he expected something to happen.

A colorful man barged out of the door, looking around. "Where is he? Who's so rich they could buy Jack a car he doesn't want?" he asked.

From where Blair stood, he could see the man's nails were purple, just like the eye shadow around his eyes. He was pretty in a delicate kind of way.

Jack groaned. "I don't need any of you to stand there. Can you go back inside, please?"

"No way," the colorful man said. "We want to know what's happening."

"I don't want to tell you," Jack said with a pout.

"Too bad. We're your family."

"You're not my brother. You're my brother's mate."

The man crossed his arms over his chest and glared. "And that doesn't make me family?"

"Please, Leon. I can't deal with this right now."

Leon's expression softened, but he wasn't done. "Fine. But we'll all be inside waiting to meet this man who bought you a car." He looked Blair up and down. "I have to say, not bad, Jack."

Jack made a strangled sound. "I have no idea what you're talking about," he protested.

"Sure you don't. Well, whoever you are, mystery man, I look forward to meeting you officially."

He was talking to Blair, and while Blair wasn't sure how to react, he raised a hand and waved at Leon. "I'm looking forward to meeting all of you, too," he said.

"Don't encourage him," Jack said. He straightened his back and squared his shoulders. "You and I have to talk."

"We'll be inside," Jack's mother said. "Once you're done *talking*, the two of you can come inside."

"Why did you say it that way? We're just going to talk," Jack protested.

The man holding a baby snickered. "Sure you are. At least the car's big enough for you to do whatever you want to do in it."

"I'm *not* having sex with him in that car," Jack snapped.

No one seemed to hear him. One by one, they went back inside, Leon being the last one. Before stepping into the house, he peered back and winked at Blair, then closed the door, leaving Jack and Blair alone.

And Jack looked like he was ready for a fight.

Jack knew his family. He was sure they were all behind the windows, staring at him and Blair. He was pretty sure he'd seen Leon take out his phone, which meant he was texting the family members who weren't there. At this rate, everyone would arrive in the next half-hour, which meant Jack had to be quick. If he wanted to get Blair out of here before the rest of his family met him, he had to start yelling at him now.

He crossed his arms over his chest and glared at Blair. "What were you thinking?"

Blair seemed lost and puzzled by Jack's anger. He probably was. From what Jack had gathered, he had more than enough money to afford to buy Jack a car and not worry about how much it cost.

And Jack was tempted to accept the gift. He needed a car, and this way, he wouldn't have to worry about the cost. It was also a new car, which meant he wouldn't be visiting the mechanic's shop anytime soon. Accepting the car would lift a huge weight from his shoulders, and it was so fucking tempting to say yes.

But doing so would feel like saying yes to Blair, and Jack wasn't ready to do that.

Blair stepped closer. Jack had to resist the urge to step back. He wanted to throw himself into his mate's arms and accept the gift, drag him inside, or maybe even into the car like Leon had suggested. It was odd to feel so drawn to someone he didn't know.

Right now, he hated the mate bond.

"I apologize if I did something you dislike," Blair said.

"But you don't understand." It wasn't a question. Jack could see it as plainly as Blair's nose in the middle of his face.

"I don't," Blair agreed. "You needed a car, and I could buy it. Why shouldn't I have?"

"Because people don't buy cars as if they're flowers."

Blair perked up. "You want flowers? I can buy them for you."

"I don't want flowers, and I don't want the car." But Jack

had no doubt that Blair could buy him an entire flower shop if he wished for it. He had to be careful what he said.

"Maybe you don't want it, but you need it."

Jack glared. He seemed to be doing a lot of that when he was with Blair. Although, to be honest, he glared a lot even when he was with other people, especially his family. "I'll find another way to get around. Besides, I bought my old car myself. I can do the same now."

"Why would you if you don't have to? Please, help me understand. You're my mate. You need a car, and I could give you one. Why is that so bad?"

Jack barely knew anything about Blair, but he could already tell he was the kind of person who threw money at problems and expected them to be solved. In this case, he wasn't wrong. Buying a car *had* solved Jack's problems, but it had also created new ones.

Jack hadn't known what to do with Blair, and he still didn't, but now, he felt like he couldn't just ignore his mate and tell him to fuck off. That meant he'd have to talk to Blair, and the thought made him uneasy.

He didn't want to owe Blair anything. He didn't want Blair to have power over him.

But if they had a relationship, Blair would have all the power. That much was obvious. Jack didn't know how to deal with that, either, and he didn't know where to start. Would Blair take the car back if Jack kept pushing? Jack was stubborn, but he could tell from Blair's expression that he wasn't the only one.

"Did you buy the car so I'd give you a chance?" he asked.

Blair blinked. "I got you the car because you need it."

"So you're not trying to buy your way into my life?"

"I didn't think I needed to do that. We're mates. I know you said you needed time, but what's there to think about?"

Jack raked a hand through his hair. He didn't want to yell

at Blair, but he was reaching the end of his patience. "Have you never thought that maybe not everyone wants to meet their mate?"

Blair seemed flabbergasted. "Why wouldn't you want to meet your mate? I've been waiting to meet you all my life. None of the relationships I've had stand up to the one the two of us will have."

"There's nothing that says we have to be together, though."

"There isn't, but why wouldn't you want to be with me?"

Jack snorted. "Maybe because you're acting as if I don't know my own mind?"

Unfortunately for Jack, before he could say anything else and before Blair could answer, a car Jack knew very well turned the corner and stopped in front of the house. He held his breath as he watched Andy and Curtis climb out. Their expressions said that Leon had already texted them and they'd come with only one purpose in mind — to meet Blair.

Jack didn't want to tell them about his mate, but he didn't see how to avoid it. He could also see that Blair would probably blurt out the fact that they were mates if Jack didn't mention it. And since Jack knew that eventually his family would find out anyway, he decided he might as well tell them what was happening. Maybe if they knew Blair was his mate, they'd understand better why he was freaking out.

He wasn't the only one of his brothers who hadn't wanted to meet his mate. Laurie hadn't, either, but he was like a different person with Alexis. He was at peace and much happier than he'd been when he'd claimed he never wanted to meet his mate.

Could the same go for Jack? Jack doubted it, but he was sure Laurie had, too. Maybe he should give Blair a chance, but that didn't make the car disappear.

"Hi," Curtis said as he neared Blair. He sounded out of breath, which made Jack roll his eyes. His brothers were ridiculous.

Blair was more hesitant as he looked from Jack to Curtis. Jack sighed and waved between the two of them. "Curtis, this is Blair. Blair, this is Curtis, one of my brothers."

"What am I? Chopped liver?" Andy protested.

"And this is Andy, yet another one of my brothers."

Blair's expression smoothed out, and he shook both their hands. He looked at ease doing that, which reminded Jack just how different they were.

"So you're the car guy," Andy said.

"I suppose you could call me that," Blair agreed. His gaze flicked to Jack again. "But I was hoping you'd call me something else."

Jack groaned and buried his face into his hands. What the fuck had he done to be saddled with his family and Blair? "Blair's my mate," he blurted out.

All four of them stayed silent for a moment, but that didn't last long. Andy strode toward Jack, grabbed his shoulders, and forced him to look at him. "Can you repeat that?"

Jack scowled at his brother. "I don't see why I should. You heard me the first time. And yes, you can tell everyone who's spying on us from the windows when you go inside. Just make sure they don't come out. Blair and I aren't done talking."

Andy stared for a moment before nodding. "All right. I'll make sure no one bothers you." He leaned closer and lowered his voice. "But give him a chance. He's not just a random guy. He's your mate."

"Who thought it was a good idea to buy me a car when we met *yesterday.*"

"Okay, so maybe he's a bit heavy-handed. But the two of you don't know each other. He won't realize he shouldn't have done that if you don't give him a chance to get to know you."

And he was right, but Jack wasn't sure he could give Blair what he wanted.

He wasn't even sure what *he* wanted, after all.

Blair had wanted to meet Jack's family, but he hadn't expected it to happen this way. Luckily, it seemed like Curtis and Andy were accepting of the fact that he and Jack were mates, but the problem was that Jack wasn't.

Blair watched as Andy and Jack had a quiet conversation. He'd almost forgotten that Curtis was standing there, too, when the man moved even closer, knocking their shoulders together. It was a shocking show of acceptance from someone he didn't know.

"They live together, you know?" Curtis said. "They're very close, maybe the closest of all brothers. Well, except Sean and Hugh, but they're twins."

"Jack told me there are seven of you."

"There are. Hugh and Sean are the oldest. I come after them, then after me are Richie, Jack, Andy, and Laurie, in that order."

That was a lot of names to remember. "I saw several brothers earlier when I arrived."

"Oh, I don't think those were all brothers. You have to think of our mates, too."

"So Jack isn't the first of you to find his mate?"

Curtis chuckled and shook his head. "He's second to last. With you in the picture, Andy's the only one who's still single."

"That's a lot of people in one family."

"It is, and I'm sure you'll be overwhelmed. All the mates are in the beginning. But you'll be fine."

Blair wasn't too sure about that. "Only if Jack wants me in his life."

Curtis paused. It looked like the conversation between Andy and Jack was coming to an end, but Blair desperately wanted to know what Curtis had to say. At this point, every single tip would help deal with Jack.

"Jack is prickly," Curtis eventually said. "I think it comes from growing up with so many brothers. Especially when we were younger, we teased each other mercilessly. That hasn't stopped, either. But most of us have mellowed. And of course, now we have our mates, so we don't spend as much time with our parents as we used to. Jack and Andy do, though. They seem always to be here, and I think that meeting you rankled Jack because things will have to change. He was talking about that at dinner a few days ago."

"He doesn't want his life to change?"

"He never does. He should have bought a new car a while ago, but he didn't want to change cars. He doesn't like change in general, and I think that's why he's freaking out so badly over your presence in his life. The only advice I can give you is to give him time and space. Eventually, he'll come around."

Curtis seemed convinced of what he was saying, but Blair wasn't. It was a huge change for anyone to meet their mate, but Jack seemed to be freaking out over it. Blair didn't know how to fix it, or even if he could.

"You should head inside," Jack said, his tone uncompromising as he glared at Curtis.

Curtis snickered, gave Blair a little wave, and followed Andy up the porch steps. Blair watched them disappear into the house, knowing they were about to tell the others that Jack had met his mate.

If Jack didn't want Blair in his life, why had he told his brothers who he was? It would have been easier for him to find another explanation, yet he hadn't even hesitated. Jack was complicated, and the thought of trying to untangle his thoughts made Blair's head hurt.

That wouldn't stop him from trying.

"You have to take the car back," Jack said. He held out his hand, and Blair realized he was trying to give him the keys.

Blair took a step back. "I won't. It's your gift. It's your car."

"No, it's not. It's a car you bought for me without even talking to me about it."

"We can talk about it now. Why are you so opposed to me giving you a car? You need it, and I can afford it. Isn't that what mates do?"

"What's going to happen if I give you a chance? What will you do next? Buy me a house? Pay all my bills?"

Blair almost said, *yes* because, once again, he could afford it. Something in Jack's expression gave him pause, though, and he took a moment to find the right words. "I'm sure you can pay your bills on your own."

Jack snorted. "I've been doing it since I left home, so yes. But you can't do this. You can't decide what I need and buy it for me. It feels like you're trying to buy my affection, and I don't want that."

"I'm just trying to make your life easier."

Jack shook his head. "No one can do that. Besides, my life isn't complicated, or at least, it wasn't until you barged into it." He held out the keys again. "Take them. I can't take the car."

But Blair still didn't reach for the keys. He understood Jack didn't want him to buy his affection, but it didn't mean he couldn't give him a car. "You need it."

"I need a million dollars, yet you're not about to give it to me."

"I could."

"Then you don't understand. I don't want anything from you. I can stand on my own two feet like I've been doing since I left home, and that's not about to change because I met you."

Jack was getting angry, and Blair didn't want him to. "You

told your brothers we're mates."

Jack blinked. "What does that have to do with anything?"

"I thought you wouldn't. I thought you didn't want me and that you were rejecting me. Yet you told them without hesitation."

"They would have found out eventually anyway. Besides, they're all spying on us, and after they found out you bought me a car, they know you're important to me."

"Am I?" Because Blair wasn't sure. Jack still sounded like he was rejecting him, and it had nothing to do with the car.

"I don't know. I suppose you are, since you're my mate."

"And if you reject me, won't they have something to say about it?"

"They have something to say about everything. I just need time, okay? And don't buy me another car. I can't accept this one, and I won't accept another." When Blair still didn't take the keys, Jack dropped them on the ground in front of him. He shook his head and stepped away. "Don't follow me. I need to take a walk and be on my own."

Blair stared at the keys. He wanted to go after Jack. They'd talked, but they hadn't solved anything. Jack had yelled at him, told him he didn't want the car, and left.

How were they supposed to be together like this? Jack was stubborn, and he wouldn't listen to anything Blair tried to explain. Blair would be the first to admit that he wasn't perfect and that he'd probably made a mistake, but Jack was uncompromising, which would be a problem if they decided to try to be together.

But would they?

The front door opened, but Blair didn't look at whoever was coming. He kept his focus on Jack, who was walking down the sidewalk, and who never peered back at him.

"Give him time," Andy said as he crouched to pick up the keys. To Blair's surprise, he didn't give them to him. Instead, he pushed them into his jeans' pocket.

"I don't know if time will help," he said.

"You don't know my brother. He's like a hedgehog, all prickly and shit, but deep inside, he's soft. He's terrified of what's going to happen if he welcomes you into his life, but he will eventually. He'll realize he's happier with you than without you."

"Do you have any suggestions as to what I could do?"

"First, don't buy him expensive shit again. I'll make sure he takes the car, but you'd be pushing your luck if you bought him something else."

"But I can afford it."

"I'm sure you can, but it doesn't mean Jack wants you to be his sugar daddy."

Blair jerked back at the words. "That's not what I was trying to do."

"I never said it was, but I'm pretty sure that's how Jack views all of this. Still, he needs the car, and he'll accept it eventually, but don't use your credit card again."

"What am I supposed to do, then?" Because this was what Blair had done every time he had a relationship. When he and the people he was with fought, he bought them gifts. That was usually enough to make peace, at least for a little while.

Andy looked at him like he was sorry, although Blair didn't understand why he should be.

"You have his phone number?" Andy asked.

"I do."

"Then call him. Text him. Make yourself more approachable. Jack doesn't know anything about you except for the fact that you have enough money to buy him a car without thinking about it. Make yourself human, tell him about you and what you like and dislike. Make him fall in love with you little by little."

Blair could do that. He *wanted* to do it.

But he wasn't entirely sure it would work, and that worried him.

CHAPTER FOUR

Jack's phone vibrated on the coffee table. He glared at it, but he didn't rise from the couch to answer. Instead, he let it ring, sighing in relief when it stopped.

"Who was that?" Andy asked from the other side of the couch.

"No clue."

Andy arched a brow. "That's bullshit. It was Blair, wasn't it?"

It had been a few days since Blair bought the car, tried to convince Jack to accept it, and left without the keys. Andy had told Jack he was being an idiot, but Jack hadn't driven the car yet, and he didn't think he would. He'd told Blair he couldn't accept the car, and he hadn't been lying.

But finding a ride to and from work every day was hell.

He was pretty sure his entire family was conspiring against him. Every time he asked someone for a ride, they either had something urgent to do, or their car wasn't working well. What were the odds of that happening every time to all *thirteen* people in Jack's family? No, they were trying to push him to accept Blair's gift, which of course, made him want to accept it even less.

Even though he needed it.

Andy set down the bowl of popcorn they'd been sharing, cleaned his hands on his jeans, and paused the movie.

Jack hadn't been watching, anyway. Thankfully, it was an old movie they'd both seen several times already, so he wouldn't be missing anything.

Andy turned on the couch to face Jack, and Jack knew he was in for an intervention. He supposed he should consider himself lucky it was only Andy and not half of his family. He knew for sure that several of them wanted to talk to him about Blair, and the only reason they hadn't was that he glared at them every time they tried.

"Why aren't you talking to Blair?" Andy asked.

"Because I don't want to."

Andy rolled his eyes. "Of course you don't. You're Jack, cold and alone on his island. You don't need anyone, and you don't *want* anyone."

Jack blinked. Was that how his brother saw him? "I never said I didn't need anyone."

"Maybe not in words, but you've been proclaiming you didn't want to meet your mate every time we talked about it, and now that you've met him, you're behaving like you don't want him. I'm surprised Blair's still calling you, to be honest. You've been ignoring him for the past two days."

"You know what he did. I don't want to talk to him."

"He bought you a car. Why did he do it, though?"

"There's no way for me to know."

"And that's bullshit again. He told you why he bought the car. He got it for you because he knew you needed it. Do you know how many people wish they could have someone like that in their life? Someone who saw what they needed and provided it without having to talk or fight about it?"

"He's trying to buy me."

Andy reached out and slapped the back of Jack's head so quickly that Jack didn't have the time to push him away. Jack scowled at his brother and rubbed the spot, even though it didn't hurt. It was just that Andy didn't hit him — Andy didn't hit anyone. Even when they were kids, he never wrestled with the rest of them.

"What did you do that for?" Jack asked.

"I felt like someone needed to do it. You're being an ass-hole."

"Is that any different from how I usually am?"

Andy sighed and looked at the ceiling as if he were gathering his patience. "No, it's not. But this situation is different. Blair isn't just a guy. He's your mate, and you're not even giving him a chance."

"I just don't want his car. How is that bad?"

"It has nothing to do with the car. If it had been just that, it wouldn't be a problem, but you're avoiding his phone calls. Have you talked to him since that day? Or are you using the car as an excuse so you don't have to talk to him?"

That *was* what Jack had been doing. He was terrified of talking to Blair, and he was using his anger because of the car as a reason not to do it. His brother knew him too well, and the same went for most of his family. "What am I supposed to say to him? I told him I didn't want the car, and he still left it with me. He doesn't respect my wishes."

Andy rolled his eyes. "That's because I told him not to. Don't be an idiot. You need a car, and it's either taking the one Blair bought you or accepting help from Mom and Dad. Why shouldn't you take the car your mate picked out for you? It's a good car, expensive but not too much, and it will serve you well. And this way, you won't have to beg for rides two times a day."

Jack looked away. He felt a bit better now that he knew Andy had insisted Blair not take the car back, but he still had no clue what to do. He didn't do this kind of thing. He didn't do relationships. Most people found him too abrasive to spend any length of time with him, and he couldn't say he blamed them. He was abrasive on purpose. He didn't need people in his life, not when he already had his family.

Andy sighed heavily and reached out to pat Jack's knee. "I know you didn't want your life to change and that you're terrified that now that you've met Blair, it will."

"You saw him," Jack croaked out. "He's rich, and he's here on a business trip. What do you think will happen if I give him a chance? He'll want me to move to wherever he lives, and I'll have to leave you and everyone else behind. He won't want me to work at the hardware store anymore, and I won't be able to because I'll have to move away." And the thought of doing that broke Jack's heart.

Maybe he did want to be with Blair. Maybe now that he'd met his mate, he wanted to give him a chance. But Blair didn't live here. He wouldn't be in town for long—if he hadn't left already—and what would they do then?

There was no denying the fact that Blair's job earned him a lot more money than Jack's, which meant he would want Jack to move in with him in the city. What would Jack do, then?

"Have you talked to him about this?" Andy asked.

"I haven't talked to him at all."

"Then don't start worrying about it before you even know what he wants."

"Why would he want to stay here?"

"I won't deny I suspect you're right, but you never know. Besides, he didn't strike me as someone who looks down on your job at the hardware store. But you won't know what he wants until you talk to him. You can't fix anything if you don't do that. And think about it. How will you feel when Blair gives up and goes back home and never calls you again? I know you think you're being strong by ignoring him and that you believe you'll be relieved when he finally goes, but I don't believe that's going to happen. I think once Blair gives up, you'll be destroyed, and you'll regret all of this."

Jack wanted to tell his brother he wouldn't, but there was no way for him to know, was there?

Jack's phone vibrated again. This time it was a text, but he stared at it as if it were a snake about to bite him. Andy huffed and reached for it, but Jack snatched it before he could look at the text. He swallowed and stared at the screen for a moment, then he took a deep breath and unlocked it.

Andy was right. Jack could ignore the situation and wait until Blair left, but was that really what he wanted to do? Would he regret it if he did?

It was Blair again, of course, and Jack hesitated only a moment before hitting the text so he could read it.

I'm heading home soon. I have to be at a fundraising party the day after tomorrow, so I can't afford to stay, especially when my business trip is over. I'd like for you to come with me and be my date at that party.

What was Jack supposed to say to that? He didn't know, and before he could think better of it, he hit Blair's number to call him.

Blair was surprised to see Jack's name on his phone when it rang. He hadn't expected Jack to answer his text, let alone call him. He wasn't sure what was about to happen, but he was ready for anything if it meant Jack said yes to coming with him and attending the party.

Blair didn't know what else to do with Jack. He'd left the car keys with Jack's brother, and he'd thought he'd hear from his mate that same evening, or maybe the day after that. When Jack hadn't called, Blair had, but Jack had never answered.

But now he was calling, and Blair had every intention of taking advantage of that. Whatever Jack was about to tell him, Blair could deal with it and make the most out of it.

Or at least, he hoped so.

"Hello," he said.

There was a moment of silence as if Jack hadn't expected Blair to answer, or maybe as if he was trying to gather his thoughts and think about something to say. "Why are you calling?" Jack asked.

Blair leaned against the headboard of his bed. The hotel room was nice, but nothing like his apartment back in the city. He couldn't say he minded, though. He liked being close to Jack, even though Jack didn't want to see him. "You were the one who called me," he pointed out.

"That's not what I meant. Why do you keep calling me?"

"People usually do that because they want to talk."

"So you want to talk to me?"

"I'd appreciate it, yes. It's hard to get to know your mate when he won't answer his phone and talk to you."

The silence between them was heavier this time. Blair hoped he hadn't scared Jack into hanging up, and he breathed out in relief when Jack's voice came again.

"Why do you want me to go to the party with you?"

"Because you're my mate. Why should I bring someone else when I have you?"

"That's it? There's no other reason?"

Blair could tell he had to be careful with how he answered, but the problem was that he had no idea what was going through Jack's mind. No matter how hard he tried, he always seemed to say or do the wrong thing when it came to his mate, and he wasn't used to that. He hated not having a secure footing, and even more so not knowing the right thing to say.

"You're my mate," he said slowly. "I'd like you to see the city I live in and my home. I'd like you to meet my parents, and I want everyone to meet you as my boyfriend. I would introduce you as my mate, but not every client and person we deal with is a shifter, so boyfriend will have to do." Unless Blair could introduce Jack as his husband, but he knew better than suggesting that.

"I can't come," Jack said.

Blair had expected that, but he'd hoped that the answer would be yes since Jack was calling. He was disappointed, but he could tell that Jack wouldn't change his mind no matter how much he pushed or how many times he asked. Blair was stubborn, but his mate was even more so.

Blair was hurt, and he didn't understand why Jack was so contrary. Blair hadn't asked him to marry him and move in with him. He'd just mentioned that he'd like Jack to see where he lived and meet his family, yet, it sounded like he'd asked Jack to throw himself off a bridge.

Would spending time with him be so bad? Jack didn't want him as a mate, but was it personal? Did Jack not want a mate, or did he not want Blair in particular?

Apart from the car, Blair couldn't think of anything he'd done that would cause Jack to push him away like this. But Jack had been horrified at the fact that they were mates since the moment they'd met, so maybe it didn't have anything to do with Blair personally.

Andy had mentioned that Jack didn't want his life to change, and there was no bigger change than meeting your mate. Some things would change for both of them, but for one of them even more. They lived in two different places, which meant that if they wanted to be together, one of them would have to move.

Maybe that was what scared Jack. Blair couldn't say he'd be happy to leave his family behind, but he wouldn't mind living in Jack's town. It was much smaller than what he was used to, but if it meant being with Jack, he'd move tomorrow.

He was pretty sure that telling Jack that would send him running, though, so he kept it to himself.

"I understand," he said slowly. But he wasn't done pushing. Something told him that maybe, in the end, Jack would say yes if he pushed enough. It wasn't like there was anything else he could do, anyway. If he stopped pushing, Jack would say no. If he kept pushing, Jack might continue to say no, or he might say yes. He might also be angry, but Blair didn't care about that right now.

"You do?" Jack asked, sounding surprised.

"Of course. We only met a few days ago, and it's understandable that you're not ready to meet my family. Unfortunately, that means I'll have to say yes to my mother's offer of setting me up on a date with one of her friends' sons."

"What are you talking about?"

Blair made himself more comfortable. He was pretty sure Jack was getting angry. While typically, he would have thought it was a bad thing, he wasn't sure that was true in this case. "My parents are worried about me. They think I work too much and don't have enough time to live, so my mother offered to set me up on a date for this party. She knows this man, and she thinks he'll be good for me. She's been pushing me to say yes, but I held off because I met you. I didn't tell her about you because I didn't know what you'd say, but she won't take no for an answer any longer if I don't have a good explanation for her."

"And you can't tell her you met your mate?"

"I could, but what would it solve? You don't want me. You don't want to go to the party with me. Whether or not I met you, it hasn't changed anything in my life."

That was a lie. It had changed everything, even though it wasn't in a tangible way. But even after what he'd said about his blind date, Blair didn't want to spook Jack. He didn't want to send him running, and he hoped that what he was doing wouldn't make that happen.

"So that's it? I say no to going to this party with you, and you give up on me?" Jack snapped. He was angry, and from the sound of it, getting angrier with every word.

Blair sat up. It took a lot to piss him off, but Jack was pushing all his limits. "What do you want me to do? I've been trying to call and text you for the past few days, and you've ignored me. To me, it's a good sign that you don't want to be with me. Should I continue insisting? Because even now that you've called me, it was only to reject my offer. What am I supposed to do with that? What am I supposed to think?"

"You're supposed to fight for me!" Jack was yelling now.

There was a lot of emotion in his voice, which surprised Blair. Until now, Jack had been fairly cold in their interactions, but he sounded like he was losing it.

"Is it a fight if you already know you'll reject me at the end?" Blair asked. He was suddenly tired and weary, and he didn't want to fight with Jack.

"Fuck you!"

Those were Jack's last words before he hung up. Blair slowly lowered the phone and looked at the screen until it turned dark. He supposed that answered his question about whether or not Jack would ever want to be with him. He'd known this could be a possibility, and he still had some hope, but for now, things were over.

Blair had to go home and deal with the work that awaited him there, go to the party, and see his family. He could worry about Jack once all of that was over.

But he already knew he wouldn't be able to stop thinking about his mate. How could he, when Jack was his life, but he wasn't the same for Jack?

Jack was pissed, and he wanted to hit something. Since the only person available was his brother, he settled for throwing his phone onto the couch and pacing back and forth between the coffee table and the TV. Andy was still on the couch, staring at Jack with a bemused expression.

Jack stopped and glared at his brother. "There. Happy? I called him, and you heard the result of that. I told you it would be a mess, and I was right."

Andy bit his lower lip as if he had something to say but wasn't sure whether or not he should say it. That was generally how his family felt when it came to telling Jack that he was an idiot, so he knew what was coming.

"I can't say I'm surprised he reacted the way he did. If that's how you listen to what people have to say and give them a chance, I understand why all your boyfriends dumped you."

"Blair isn't my boyfriend," Jack snapped.

"Maybe not, but he's something much more important. You're supposed to give him a chance, and instead, you basically told him to fuck off."

"I just said I didn't want to go to the party. Would you go, considering the situation? Going to that party would mean being away and probably staying with him and meeting his family."

"He already met yours, or at least part of it. Why can't you meet his?"

Because it would make everything more real. Because meeting Blair's family would mean that they were one step closer to being in a relationship, and Jack's life was one step closer to changing entirely.

That was why he couldn't give in to Blair. That was why he couldn't say yes.

But fuck, he wanted to.

Andy was right. If Jack wanted to have a chance with Blair, he'd have to compromise. His life would change, and he'd have to learn to deal with it. What was the alternative? Jack could stay here, continue living with his brother, and think about the mate he rejected. What would Blair do when Jack told him he didn't want to see him ever again? He'd go back home, to his job and apartment, to his family, and the blind date his mother was organizing for him.

The thought of Blair with another man made Jack want to punch something. He didn't want his mate to go on a date with anyone else. He didn't want his mate to *look* at anyone else. But could Jack ask that of him when he was the one who'd rejected Blair?

Jack buried his face in his hands and screamed. The sound was muffled, but he suspected his neighbors would still have something to say about it. He didn't care, though. He was frustrated and angry and didn't know what to do, and he needed to scream.

When he lowered his hands, Andy was staring at him. "Got that out of your system?" he asked.

Jack grabbed his phone and flopped onto the couch. "What am I supposed to do?"

Andy's expression shifted to something more serious. "It depends on what you want. You've met your mate. Most people would be happy about that, but you aren't. No one wants you to say yes to Blair just because he's your mate if it means you'll be unhappy. Would being with him be that bad, though?"

"I'm scared," Jack whispered. Actually, he was terrified. "I don't know what to do with a mate. I don't want my life to change."

"But it will, whether or not you say yes to Blair. What do you think will happen if you tell him to leave and never come back? You won't be able to forget that you've met your mate. You'll continue thinking about him, and you'll wonder what he's doing in the city. Wouldn't it be best for you to say yes to him?"

"What if he wants me to move and live in the city? I'd have to leave you and my job behind."

"But you wouldn't be moving to another continent. You don't even know where Blair's from, anyway. It might not be as far as you fear."

"It would still be far enough that I wouldn't be able to work at the hardware store and live with you."

Andy's smile was sad. "Were you thinking about living

with me for the rest of our lives? We always knew it was temporary. I can't say I wouldn't be sad being unable to see you every day, but if being with Blair makes you happy, I'd accept it. We all would."

But every one of Jack's brothers lived in town with their mate. Their parents had never had to say goodbye to one of their kids, not for the long run. Curtis had left for a while, as had Richie, but they'd both come back.

Could Jack do that, too? Would Blair even consider the idea of moving to a small town? There was no denying that Blair's job was more important than Jack's. Jack just worked at the hardware store. He earned decent money, but it was nowhere near what Blair earned. Jack suspected that Blair would support him if he asked, and he wouldn't have to work another day in his life.

Not that he wanted to do that. He despised the thought of Blair paying for everything, and even if he moved, he'd try finding another job. The problem was that he wasn't sure what he'd be able to find. He'd never done anything beyond graduating from high school and working at the store. What job could he get in the city?

But what was the alternative? It was Blair going back home, saying yes to the date with whoever his mother wanted him to meet, and probably eventually marrying that guy. If not that one, another one anyway. Jack suspected that if he said no and allowed Blair to go home by himself, he'd never see him again. Blair had tried to be with him. He'd tried to communicate, to find a way to work with Jack, but Jack had rejected him and every single attempt at a conversation, let alone a relationship. No matter how much patience Blair had, it wasn't infinite, and Jack suspected he was reaching the end of it.

The ball was in his court. He could decide to be stubborn about this, keep saying no, and watch Blair leave and never come back. That was what he should do, considering everything, but he found that he couldn't.

Despite everything—despite his fears—he didn't want to lose Blair.

"You don't have to marry him just because you go to the party with him," Andy said, always the voice of reason. "And you don't have to move in with him just because you're going to the city to attend the party. Things might not work between you in the end, but you'll never know if you don't give it a chance. I don't think Blair deserves to be treated the way you've been treating him. He's been trying, and even though he's gotten some things wrong, he can't understand because you won't tell him. You're not giving him and the two of you a chance, and I think you'll regret it if you don't."

Jack looked at his brother. "What will happen if I say yes and go? What if things work between us and I have to leave?"

"Then you leave. If you want to be with Blair, and he wants to be with you and make you happy, you should follow that happiness. I know you're scared and that you don't want to have to move away, but it might happen, and you'll have to deal with it. But it might also not be forever. Besides, even if you don't live here, you won't get rid of us. We're your family, which means we'll be in your life until you die." Andy grinned. "Whether you want us to be or not."

Jack chuckled. "I know I won't lose you. I just don't want anything to change. I like my life the way it is."

"I know you do, but you might like your life even more with Blair in it. Besides, there's nothing to say that you *have* to move. You can't know any of this until you talk to him, and that's not going to happen if you keep saying no and yelling at him when you talk."

Andy was right, and Jack knew what he had to do.

He unlocked his phone and pulled up the text Blair had sent him earlier.

When Blair's phone vibrated, he almost didn't check it. The only reason he did was that it could be his parents or Lisa, and they'd worry if he didn't answer. But it was his personal cell, so it wasn't work, which was a relief, because he wasn't up to dealing with anything related to that right now.

Blair was angry. He wished Jack would listen to him, and he didn't understand why he wasn't willing even to do that. On the other hand, he was also sad, and if Jack had called him to apologize, he'd have accepted that apology in a second.

But Jack wouldn't call. He didn't seem the type, and he was stubborn as a mule. Blair didn't usually have a problem with people like that, but he'd never dealt with someone so stubborn in his personal life. Usually it was work, and it was easy to deal with that. Jack was something Blair had never dealt with, though, and he didn't know where to start. It felt like every time he tried something, it was a mistake, and it ended up blowing up in his face.

He grabbed the phone from the bed and peered at the screen, his eyes widening when he saw Jack's name on it. He quickly unlocked it, opened the text, and read it, his heart racing as he wondered if it was Jack rejecting him or if he'd changed his mind.

I'll come.

That was it. Blair had expected and hoped for something more, but he was still shocked that Jack had reached out to him, and even more so at the meaning of the text. Surely, it couldn't mean what he thought it meant?

What do you mean? he texted back.

He wanted to call, but he was afraid of freaking Jack out. For some reason, Jack had decided he wanted to come to the party with Blair, and Blair had no intention of doing anything that would make him change his mind.

It took way too long for Jack to answer, and Blair stared at the screen the entire time. He could see the three dots dancing on his screen, which meant that Jack was probably writing stuff, erasing it, and writing again. In the end, he only got a few words in answer.

To the party.

Blair snorted. That was all Jack could come up with? *It took you five minutes to write three words?* he texted, hoping he wouldn't make Jack snap.

You're lucky you got an answer at all because it was obvious what I was talking about. I'm coming to your party. Happy?

Blair was. He couldn't stop smiling, even as he started typing the details Jack would need to know about the fundraising. *I'm leaving town tomorrow. It's not far, so I can come and pick you up the day after that.*

You don't have to. I'll drive.

That made Blair grin even wider. *In your new car?* He could imagine Jack was glaring at the screen, but if he wanted to come to the city on his own, he'd have to drive the car.

Yes, in my new car. And if you don't stop being smug, I'll punch you the next time I see you.

I'm not into punching, but I wouldn't mind some spanking if you really have to take your anger out on me, Blair answered. He was probably pushing things a bit too much, but he was finally talking to Jack, even if it was only through texts. He couldn't believe that Jack was changing his mind, and he wanted to show Jack a bit of his personality. He felt like so far he hadn't been able to, mostly because Jack wouldn't have listened to him.

What else do I need to know? Jack asked without saying anything about the spanking thing.

Blair could deal with that. *Bring a suit. It's a fundraising dinner, but no one will expect you to donate money. It's more for companies and other wealthy people, so you don't have to worry about that. I have to warn you that you'll meet my family, though. They'll be at the party with me.* And they'd be stunned that Blair had

found someone, especially when he told them it was his mate.
He couldn't wait.

I don't have a suit, was Jack's answer.

Blair blinked. He supposed he shouldn't have assumed. He
lived in suits, wearing them most days of the week, but with
Jack working at the hardware store, it would make sense he
didn't have one. *I'll get you one.*

Don't spend any more money on me.

Of course that was Jack's answer. *Would you rather come in
jeans and a t-shirt? Because it's not a problem for me if you do that.*

But I'll stand out. The three dots danced again. *Fine. You can
buy me a suit and whatever else I need to wear that evening. But
that's it.*

I promise I won't buy you anything expensive.

*I said that was it. I didn't say anything about expensive, and I
don't want you to buy me anything else, period.*

Blair grinned and quickly texted Jack where the party
would be and when it started. Jack had said he'd drive there,
which meant they'd meet at the party. Blair wished Jack
would come to his apartment and maybe spend the night, but
he supposed he'd have more chances of that happening after
the party than before. As long as everything went well, Blair
hoped he'd be going home with Jack after the fundraiser and
that Jack would spend the night with him and possibly, the
rest of his life.

When Jack stopped answering after Blair had told him everything he needed to know about the party and gotten Jack's
size for the suit, Blair dialed his mother's number. She needed
to know he was coming with Jack so she wouldn't organize
that blind date.

"Blair," she answered. She sounded like she was smiling.
"Are you already back in the city?"

"Not yet. It's my last night here, so I'll be back tomorrow. I
could have driven now, but I have something to do." More
like Blair didn't want to leave the town because he didn't

want to be away from Jack.

He hadn't been supposed to stay in town at all. With only a one-hour drive between this place and his home, he could have easily gone back after everything was said and done. But Jack was here, which meant that was where Blair wanted to be. Besides, he liked this little town. It was nothing like he was used to, which was part of its charm. He understood why Jack's parents had wanted to raise their children here and why all of their sons had decided to stay even once they'd become adults.

"But you'll be back in time for the party?"

"I will, which is why I called. I wanted to tell you that I have a date."

His mother sucked in a breath. "You do? Or are you only saying that because you don't want to go on that blind date? I don't have to organize it if you don't want to, you know?"

"I would have said yes, but I do have a date. He's my mate."

"Your mate?"

Blair couldn't wait for his parents to meet Jack. They would love him as much as Blair did.

Because he did. It wasn't romantic love or anything like that, not yet, but he loved how prickly and stubborn Jack was, even though it had created trouble Blair didn't know how to deal with. Jack had a strong personality, and he knew what he wanted and was ready to do anything to obtain it, maybe too much so. Blair was pretty sure that once they smoothed things out between them, though, they'd be a team against the world, and that was all he'd ever wanted from a relationship.

"His name is Jack. He agreed to come as my date, so you'll be able to meet him."

"That's wonderful. I didn't expect to hear those words from you today."

Blair laughed. "Or any day, right? But I did. I met my mate, just like you."

"And you'll be as happy as your father and me."

Blair could only pray that would be the case. He'd have to deal with Jack's prickliness first, but Jack had agreed to come to the party with him. That was a big step forward, and hopefully, it would be the first of many of them.

Whatever Jack was afraid of, whatever he wasn't willing to compromise on to be with Blair, Blair would find a way around it. He'd never put much effort in a relationship because all of the people he'd been with before had wanted something beyond being with him. It had been money, jobs, or connections, and Blair had been more than happy to give that to them, but not his love.

Jack was different. He was Blair's mate, and Blair hoped this relationship would be nothing like his previous ones. It was already different, in a way. He'd never had to push so much to have someone agree to go on a date with him.

But that was one of the things he liked about Jack. He knew what he wanted, and he didn't back down in front of anyone or anything, even when he was obviously wrong. That might be a problem if Jack didn't learn to smooth out his sharp angles, but there was time for that to happen.

Blair felt they had all the time in the world now that they'd met each other.

CHAPTER FIVE

Jack was out of place. He should have known better when he'd decided to arrive in the city early, had told Blair about it, and Blair had given him his address. He'd gone there, both excited and nervous about spending time with Blair, but the only thing he'd been able to focus on was the luxury apartment Blair lived in. Blair had insisted on giving Jack his guest room for the night after the party, and while Jack had wanted to refuse and go straight home, he hadn't.

He wasn't sure why. He should go home. He didn't belong here, with these people, and he was starting to realize that he didn't belong with Blair, either.

He looked around the room. They'd arrived early at the party held at the museum because Blair wanted to introduce Jack to his family, and Jack had been relieved when he'd seen that several people had already arrived, too. That meant there was a delay in meeting Blair's parents, and he was tempted to hide behind one of the enormous potted plants in the corner and stay there for the rest of the night. Blair would be disappointed, and he'd look for him, but Jack wasn't sure he could do this.

He looked down at himself and smoothed his suit jacket over his stomach. When it had been delivered to his parents' home, he'd wanted to send it back. He knew nothing about suits, but even he could tell it was expensive, and it had come with everything Jack would need, including shoes and a belt. Now Jack knew why Blair had required his measurements. The suit fell perfectly on his body, as if it had been made for him, and he wondered if that was the case. He supposed there hadn't been time to make the suit, but still. It was the most expensive and luxurious item of clothing he owned, and he was pretty sure he'd never wear it again. He also suspected Blair wouldn't take it back if he tried, because, well, it was his size, not Blair's.

Jack had to admit it looked good, and he didn't look out of place, but that didn't change the fact that he felt he was. It didn't change the fact that he *knew* he was.

He hadn't known what to expect from the party, and he'd been surprised when Blair had driven them to the museum. Jack liked art, but he seldom spent any time around it. Between his family and his job, he didn't get to the city more than a few times a year, if even that.

The museum looked good, but the art was strange. Apparently, Jack wasn't into modern art, but many people around him seemed to be. They fawned over the sculptures and paintings on the walls, talking about color use and metaphysical meaning, making Jack want to run away. He made sure to stay as far away from the art pieces as possible in case someone asked him what he thought about them.

A hand on the small of his back made him jerk away. He almost dropped the glass of champagne he was sipping from, but he tightened his grip on it and forced a smile on his lips when he looked at Blair.

"Everything okay?" Blair asked.

"Of course."

Blair seemed skeptical, but he was distracted by a woman gliding toward them, her hand held out as if she were a queen. She certainly looked like one, and Jack wasn't surprised to see Blair catch her hand and kiss the top of it.

What the fuck was Jack doing here? This was what he could look forward to if he decided to give his relationship with Blair a chance, and once again, it felt like a terrible idea.

He'd come because he didn't want to waste the only opportunity to be with his mate, but now, he wondered who had chosen Blair for him. If it was fate, they must have been drunk, because there was nothing in common between Jack and Blair, and Jack was pretty sure that eventually Blair would realize that.

There was no way Blair wouldn't want some of the smooth, beautiful men walking around the room. They fit perfectly in Blair's world, unlike Jack. Jack had expected everything to be nice but not so visibly expensive, and he itched to go back home. He felt like if he stayed, he'd get something dirty or break it, which would attract everyone's attention and make Blair ashamed.

"There are my parents," Blair said.

Jack's back went ramrod straight. "Where?" he asked, his mouth dry at the thought of meeting them. "You can't tell them—" he started, but a good-looking couple was on them before he could finish the sentence. He wanted to tell Blair he shouldn't tell his parents they were mates. They were bound to be disappointed, and Jack didn't want to ruin the evening for anyone.

Blair's parents were both in their early sixties, but they looked younger. His mother wore a black cocktail dress, and her hair was artfully piled on the top of her head. She wore makeup, and she was smiling, clearly happy to see Blair. Blair's father wore a suit, like every other man in the room. He wore it well, the fabric stretching across his broad shoulders. Jack could see who Blair had taken after. His features made him look like his mother, but physically, he'd taken after his father.

"There you are," Blair's mother said.

"I told you I was coming," Blair said, catching her hand and pulling her closer to kiss her cheek.

"Considering the news you gave me, I was wondering if

you'd stay home. We would have understood." She turned her attention to Jack, and Jack froze like a rabbit in front of a wolf. He swallowed, trying to say something, but he couldn't make a word pass his lips.

Blair said hello to his father. Then they too turned to Jack. A tiny frown marred Blair's expression as Blair's father held his hand out.

Jack didn't take it. He couldn't move, and besides, he and Blair had never really touched. Jack didn't want to start here, no matter how much he wanted to bury himself against Blair's chest.

How was it possible that Blair felt like the only safe person here? Why were Jack's instincts yelling at him that as long as Blair was with him, he was safe and didn't have to worry about anyone else in the room?

"Mom, Dad, this is Jack," Blair said. "As I told Mom on the phone, he's my mate."

Jack almost groaned. How would Blair explain to his parents that Jack had left and was never coming back? That they wouldn't be together, even though they were mates? Maybe he hadn't realized it would be for the best, but Jack had always known, and everything he'd seen tonight had reinforced that idea.

He didn't belong here. He didn't belong with Blair.

Still, he didn't want Blair to look bad, so he forced a smile on his lips and held out his hand. "It's a pleasure to meet you," he managed to say.

Blair's mother clasped Jack's hand with both of hers and pulled him closer until she wrapped her arms around him. Jack was startled, and he tensed, but before she could realize, she let him go. He quickly took a step back, hoping the smile was still plastered on his face.

"It's such a pleasure to meet you," she said. "We never thought Blair would find his mate, and I can't tell you how happy we are that he has."

"I'm sure," Jack whispered.

Jack's father stepped closer. "Call me Edgard, please."

Blair chuckled. "I apologize, but I'm a bit overwhelmed. Jack, these are my parents, Edgard and Matilda."

Blair was overwhelmed? Jack couldn't imagine that. He belonged here, and obviously, he belonged with his parents. Everything around them, *everyone* around them, was smooth and beautiful and luxurious. The only one who stood out was Jack, and he didn't understand how Blair didn't see it.

"I see Oliver," Blair's father said. "He told me he wanted to talk to you, and he's coming this way."

Blair grimaced and looked at Jack. "It'll be just a moment. Stay with my parents, and I'll be right back."

Jack opened his mouth to tell him he wasn't supposed to leave him alone, but Blair was already gone. Jack swallowed and eyed Blair's parents, wondering what they were supposed to talk about. It wasn't like he could tell them about his job at the hardware store.

Matilda's smile was gentle, but Jack doubted it would last long once she realized he didn't belong with her son.

"Blair hasn't told us much about you," she started. "It's made us curious. Although I suppose we'll have all the time in the world to get to know you once you move to the city."

"Blair told you I'd be moving?"

"Oh, no, but it makes sense, doesn't it?"

Jack supposed it did. He'd wondered if he'd be able to do it before he'd arrived, and he'd even decided that he just might if it meant being with Blair. But after seeing all of this, he realized he'd been right when he'd told Andy it couldn't work.

It was a miracle he hadn't run away yet, and it was taking everything he had to stay where he was. As soon as Matilda and Edgard got distracted, though, he'd slip out, and hopefully, he'd be able to find his way out of the museum. He needed to go home.

To Clifton.

"This evening isn't supposed to be about business," Blair said.

Oliver had the good taste of looking bashful. "I apologize. I just wanted to mention this to you before I forgot. You know how it is."

Blair did know how Oliver was, so he wasn't surprised the man had stopped him during the party. "It's not a problem. Make sure to email my secretary. I want all the details."

"Hopefully, I won't forget," Oliver said with a smile.

Blair was eager to go back to Jack. The problem was that once he'd managed to step away from Oliver, he was stopped by another client that he had to talk to for a few minutes, too. At least Jack was in good hands with his parents.

Blair had almost kissed Jack when he'd appeared on his doorstep wearing the suit Blair had bought him. Blair had hoped it would fit, and he'd been happy to see it did. Jack looked incredible, handsome, and strong at the same time. And if he was honest with himself, Blair couldn't wait to drag him back to his apartment and have his way with him. What would it be like to get Jack on his bed, slowly take the suit off him piece by piece, and finally have him naked?

Not that they'd talked about it. Blair had been surprised when Jack had arrived early, and he'd been glad to see him in his apartment, but he'd had so many things to do that he couldn't dedicate the time to him he deserved. The same went for the party. No matter how much Blair wanted to stick close to Jack, he had to work this party the way it should be. It was a fundraiser, and he needed to raise money.

By the time he managed to extricate himself from everyone and make his way back to his parents, he couldn't wait to see

Jack again. Jack was a breath of fresh air in the room, and Blair had never realized how much he needed that. Jack might be new here, and he might not have any idea of what was happening around him, but it was good to have something different in the room for once. It gave Blair even more incentives to do his job quickly so he'd be able to leave.

He frowned when he found his parents again and realized that Jack wasn't next to them. He snatched a glass of champagne from the tray when the waitress walked past him. Then he made his way toward them. "Where's Jack?" he asked when he reached them.

His mother looked at him with a frown. "He said he had to go to the bathroom. I'm pretty sure it was a lie, though."

Blair's stomach turned to lead. "What do you mean?"

"Well, we were talking about him moving to the city, and he looked disturbed by the conversation. I'm not sure why."

Blair knew exactly why. "Did you say anything else?"

"We talked about your job, and I asked him what he did. I was just wondering how hard it would be to get him moved here, you know? Now that you've met, you need to keep him close."

"But we haven't talked about him moving here, Mom. You dumped all of that on him, and he probably has no idea what's going on."

"Oh, I'm so sorry." Her hand flew to her throat. "I just thought that since you're mates and met several days ago, you'd have already started the process to move him here."

Blair wasn't surprised his mother assumed that Jack would be the one moving. If an outsider looked at their situation, it was the most logical thing to happen. Jack could find a job anywhere. Hell, he didn't even have to find a job. Blair would happily provide for him, and if Jack wanted, he'd never have to work another day in his life. On the other hand, it would be harder for Blair to work from Clifton. It wasn't that far from the city, though, so he supposed he could drive back and forth, but it wasn't something anyone would do if they didn't have to.

But *he* would.

But like his mother, he'd assumed that eventually Jack would move to the city. He'd imagined Jack living in the apartment with him, being there when he came home from work, welcoming and smiling and warm. He hadn't even thought about the fact that Jack might decide to stay in Clifton and ask him to move there.

"You should probably talk to him," Blair's father said. "I think I saw him leaving the room and heading to the garden."

It made sense. Even though Jack was used to being around many people, considering how big his family was, this was different. Blair had been keeping an eye on him since they'd arrived as much as he could. He'd noticed that Jack didn't talk to anyone but him, and now, his parents. He'd looked uncomfortable, and while Blair had put it up to the new suit and shoes, maybe he'd been wrong.

Maybe he'd been assuming many things about Jack and his life and their relationship, and he shouldn't have.

"I'll go," he said. "I'll see you later?"

"We'll be around here, and we'll tell Lisa to give you space," Blair's mother promised.

Blair took one last sip of champagne, set down the glass on one of the tables strategically placed around the room, and headed outside.

The air was cool, but it felt good to be away from the party. He understood why Jack had wanted to be out here. While the garden was open for any guest who wanted to take a walk, smoke, or just get some fresh air, it seemed like everyone was still inside. It was quiet, especially after Blair closed the door behind himself, and he took a moment to look around.

He wondered where Jack had gone. Was he looking at the

statues that stood at regular intervals in the garden? Or was he peering at the roses?

A movement on Blair's left made him turn around. He squinted, trying to see in the half-darkness, smiling when he noticed a foot pulling back. If he remembered correctly, there was a bench there, hidden by the shrubs, and apparently, that was where his mate was hiding.

Blair made his way toward the bench. He wasn't sure where to start or what to say to Jack. He wanted to reassure Jack that whatever had happened, it didn't matter. He wanted to apologize for what his mother had said and assumed, but he couldn't deny the fact that he'd assumed the same. There was a lot of work to do, and Blair would have to make sure he did that work. He wanted to make Jack happy, but the problem was that he didn't know *what* would make Jack happy. Unless Jack told him, it would be impossible for him to find out.

"Jack?" he called out when he'd almost reached the bench.

Jack jerked to his feet, materializing in front of Blair. He stepped away from the bench and toward Blair, but Blair raised a hand to stop him. "We can stay here for a while, if you're more comfortable. I understand this kind of party isn't for everyone and that you must have been bored."

Jack looked down at his feet. "I wouldn't say that."

But it had been obvious. Blair didn't know how to explain to Jack that he wanted him to be honest and to be himself. As it was, Jack had pulled up his mask and expected Blair not to see through it. But Blair could, at least in part.

Where was the prickly and snarky Jack he'd met in Clifton? That was who he wanted to be with. That was who his mate was, but tonight, there were no traces of him. Jack had been painfully polite and silent, and it wasn't like him.

"We can go home if you want," Blair said when he reached Jack.

"This is your job, isn't it? You shouldn't have to go home because of me."

"I'd do many things because of you, including this."

Jack shook his head. "But you shouldn't have to." He sucked in a breath and looked Blair straight in the eyes. "I can't do this, Blair."

These weren't the words Blair had wanted to hear, and his stomach felt like it dropped to his feet.

Jack could see the confusion in Blair's expression. He was pretty sure it was the first time he noticed that kind of emotion in Blair, and he was glad to see it. He was also sorry he was about to break Blair's heart, although he supposed that Blair would get over it quickly considering the situation.

Why shouldn't he? He might want to be with Jack because they were mates, but if he hadn't realized that Jack didn't belong with him, he would soon. Then he'd probably find someone else to date, maybe that guy his mother had wanted him to come to the party with, and he'd forget all about Jack.

Blair reached out, but Jack took a step back, not wanting his mate to touch him. He wasn't sure he'd be able to stand it. He'd made his decision, but it felt fragile, as if one word or touch from Blair would make Jack change his mind.

He desperately wanted to. No matter how much he tried keeping Blair at a distance, no matter what he'd said to his family, he did want to be with Blair. His entire being yearned to throw himself into Blair's arms and never leave, but he wasn't just a shifter. He couldn't listen to that instinct, not when it was so obviously wrong.

"What are you talking about?" Blair asked.

Jack gestured around them. "You have to see that this isn't my place. I don't belong here."

"This is a museum. No one belongs here."

"Don't act as if you don't understand what I'm talking about. I stand out like a sore thumb. And the only reason I haven't been kicked out is that I'm wearing a suit, and I'm your guest."

"Is it about what my mother said? Because I informed her that we haven't talked about it yet. She assumed you'd be moving, but she's the only one."

Jack chuckled darkly. "She's not. You can't tell me you didn't think I'd be the one to move here. I thought the same."

Blair took a step closer, and Jack let him. Even though he was breaking up with Blair, he still wanted his mate close. "Why did you think that?" Blair asked.

"It's obvious, isn't it? I work in a hardware store. Your job is much more important than mine, and it would be easier for me to move. I thought I might give it a try, at least until I got here."

"And you feel you don't belong."

"It's not just a feeling. I truly don't belong. This place, this suit, and these people, they're not what I'm used to."

"It doesn't mean you can't get used to having all of this in your life."

"Maybe so, but still. What am I supposed to talk to these people about? The kind of nails you need to build a house? They'd look at me like I was nuts, and I wouldn't blame them. I don't want my presence to reflect badly on you and to ruin your chances of raising money for whatever you're raising it for."

"You could never do that."

"But don't you see I already am? Your parents tried talking to me, but I had no idea what they were talking about. Your mother said something about us all going together to Polynesia this summer, and I don't even know where it is."

"But that doesn't matter."

"It does." And for the first time, Jack truly realized what it meant for him to leave his mate behind. Until now, he'd insisted he didn't want Blair. But he'd been sure that Blair would insist and push and that in the end, everything would be okay. They were mates, so it had to be that way.

But even though they were mates, they were too different. Now that Jack was here and had seen Blair's life, he couldn't imagine them finding a way to fit together.

He cleared his throat and ignored the way his eyes burned. He didn't want to cry and make this harder on Blair. "I can't move here. I can't move to the city and fit in your life, not when I'm me."

"But don't you see?" Blair reached for Jack again, and this time, Jack allowed him to take his hand. "You already fit in my life."

"I don't. You don't understand, or maybe you don't want to see the problem. It's like with the car."

Blair huffed. "What about the car?"

"You bought it just because you could. You didn't think to talk to me about it. You just went ahead, not even wondering how I'd feel when I got it. I feel like you're taking over my life. You bought me a car, you got me to come here to this party, and now, you're already planning our holidays together this summer. Do I have a say in any of it?"

"We don't have to go to Polynesia if you don't want to."

Jack wasn't sure how to make Blair understand. "We're so different. You're used to using money to get whatever you want, but that doesn't work with me. I don't want you to pay me to be with you. I don't want to move here and have you support me."

"Then you can find a job."

"Can I? Even if I could find a job at a hardware store here, can you tell your clients and your parents that's what I do for a living? I feel like you're showing off how much better than me you are, and you know what? It worked. I realized that

I'm not enough, especially after coming to this party. I saw the place you live in, the car you drive, and the people you meet every day. This isn't my place, and it never will be."

"Are you breaking up with me?"

"Can I break up with you when we were never really together?" Jack regretted not taking advantage of the time Blair had spent in Clifton. Maybe it was better this way, though. If Jack had given Blair a chance while they were home, he'd have been even more heartbroken now that he was telling Blair they couldn't be together.

"I can change," Blair said softly.

He looked as heartbroken as Jack felt. It didn't make sense. Surely, Blair had to see this was the best thing for both of them. Hadn't he realized that Jack didn't belong here? "But you shouldn't have to change."

For some reason, that seemed to get Blair's attention. His eyes narrowed, and his back straightened, and he stared at Jack. "Is that what you think? That people shouldn't have to change to be with the people they want to be with?"

"Not when it comes to mates. Aren't we supposed to be perfect for each other? It's clear we're not, which is why I think there was a mistake. Maybe it wasn't me you smelled in my car but my brother."

Blair snorted. "You mean Andy, the only one of your brothers who's still single?"

"He spends a lot of time in my car."

"But, Jack, I didn't smell your car. I smelled *you*. You might not know this, but the day your car was delivered and I came to your house, I talked to Andy after you left. He promised he'd make sure you took the car. We were close enough to touch each other then, and I'm sure he's not my mate. You are, and you're the only mate I'll ever get."

Which made the situation all the more heartbreaking, but what else could Jack do? He couldn't move here and be with

Blair, and Blair couldn't move to Clifton with him. They were stuck, and there was only one way out—breaking up.

Jack had fought his relationship with Blair every step of the way, and now, he realized he'd done the right thing. Coming here thinking that they could be together had been a mistake. Jack had given this a chance, and he could see he shouldn't have. He and Blair didn't belong together, no matter how they smelled or what they wanted.

Blair should have realized how out of place Jack was feeling. It had been obvious in the way Jack stood and behaved, but Blair had figured that was because they barely knew each other. Everything made more sense now that Jack had finally been honest with him, though. Blair knew what the problem was, and he hoped to fix things before Jack convinced himself they didn't have a chance to make it as a couple.

Blair wasn't sure where to start. He supposed the first step would be convincing Jack that he hadn't smelled Andy but him. Blair was sure of that, and he wanted Jack to be just as sure.

He inched closer, relieved when Jack didn't push him away. He'd thought Jack didn't care about him, but he could see he'd been wrong. The pain Jack felt was plain on his face, and while it was a shock to realize that Jack felt so strongly about him, Blair liked it. He'd been afraid Jack would push him away and not care what happened next. He'd worried that Jack didn't care about him and didn't want him, but now, looking at Jack, he knew the truth.

Jack wanted him as much as he wanted Jack.

Blair gently cupped Jack's cheek and rubbed his thumb on his cheekbone. "Smell me," he murmured. "That way, you'll know that you're my mate, not your brother."

Jack didn't resist when Blair pulled him closer. Blair

wrapped his arms around his mate, holding him close the way he'd been yearning to since they'd met. He was pretty sure that if he'd tried sooner, Jack would have punched him, but now, he melted in Blair's arms, clinging to him as if he were a lifeboat and Jack was about to drown.

Jack buried his face against Blair's neck. Blair felt him take a deep breath, and he did the same, sending Jack's smell to memory. There hadn't been a doubt in his mind that Jack was his mate, but it was reassuring to be able to hold him like this and breathe him in.

Jack was Blair's mate. There was no denying that, for either of them.

"What now?" Jack whispered against the skin of Blair's neck.

Blair didn't want to let him go. He wanted to continue holding Jack until Jack realized they were made for each other.

He couldn't deny he'd wondered what fate had been thinking. He doubted there was anyone more different from him than Jack, and that knowledge made it hard to be able to think of a way to make things work between them. But they were mates, and there had to be a reason for that. Blair had every intention of finding that reason and loving Jack for the rest of his life, whether Jack wanted him to or not.

Besides, he was pretty sure Jack did want him to love him. His mouth said one thing when he'd explained he needed to leave and that he didn't belong, but his expression and his eyes said something else. Jack wanted to be with Blair, even though he apparently couldn't see a way to make that happen.

Blair was used to dealing with problems and solving them to the best of his ability. He was good at it, and he had even more incentives of finding a way out of this when it came to their situation. He and Jack would be together, one way or another, and apparently, it would fall on Blair's shoulders to make sure it happened.

But first, he and Jack had a lot of work to do and things to talk about.

"Why don't we go home?" he said, leaning back so he could look at Jack.

Jack frowned. "You're supposed to be here. The party is important."

"It is, but not as important as you. Besides, my parents and my sister are here. They'll take care of everything."

"Are you sure?"

Blair wasn't used to seeing Jack so hesitant. He understood it was because Jack felt insecure, and he wanted that to change. He never wanted Jack to feel this way around him. "I'm sure. There's nothing more important than you. I need you to understand that and to remember it when you have doubts." It would be best if Blair was able to *show* Jack how much he meant, but for a start, he could say it.

Jack slowly nodded. He still looked like he didn't quite believe Blair, so Blair decided to take things into his own hands. He stepped away from Jack, but he didn't completely release him. He took his hand and pulled him along, and they walked through the garden, bypassing the room where the party was going on. They could hear the sound of music, people laughing and talking, and the light coming from the windows was enough to illuminate their path.

They walked around the building, heading toward the entrance. The man there looked surprised to see them, but he didn't hesitate when Blair asked for his car. Within a few minutes, he and Jack were slipping into it, leaving the party behind, and heading toward Blair's apartment.

"I think a lot of the problems between us exist because we haven't talked," Blair said, hoping Jack wouldn't snap. The main reason they hadn't talked was that Jack hadn't allowed them to. Ever since they'd met, Blair had been going after him, and Jack had been running.

"And that's my fault," Jack said with a snort.

"Maybe a little." At least he'd admitted it. Blair had been scared he wouldn't. "You've been avoiding me and holding up your anger as a shield between us. The problem is that I didn't understand why you were so angry until you explained that to me earlier. I never wanted you to feel like you weren't enough or like you're inferior to me. To me, all of this is just money, which isn't something I've ever had to worry about. I understand your life hasn't been that way, though, but I would have liked it if you'd told me that instead of screaming at me and stomping away. I just wanted to make your life easier, and the way to do that was to get you that car."

"I know," Jack murmured. "I think I used that as a way to keep you away. I mean, I want you to promise never to buy me something so expensive without telling me again, but I can see why you did it. To be honest, I was relieved you bought me that car, because I needed it."

Blair was glad to hear that. They had at least that out of the way, but it was just the beginning.

"So thank you," Jack continued.

"You don't have to thank me. And I promise that next time I want to buy you something expensive, I'll talk to you first. I can't do that with every single gift, though. I realize that you don't have the same easiness as me around money. But just like it would be hard for you to accept that I can pay your bills, rent, or buy you a car without even thinking about it, and that I would do it happily because it's you, you have to see my point of view. I'm used to living like this. I'm used to people wanting money and other things from me. It's just the way I do things, because it's what I'm used to."

"We're very different."

"We are, but it doesn't mean we can't work as a couple." Blair quickly added. He needed to show Jack they truly could work together. "Try to see things my way. I know you live in an apartment with your brother, but haven't you ever thought about buying your own place? Maybe a house, where you could build a family, have pets, something like that?"

"Of course I have."

When Blair quickly looked at Jack, Jack had a wistful expression on his face.

"There's this house, a few streets away from my parents. I used to walk past it every day when I was a kid, even though I didn't need to be there. It was just gorgeous, you know? It still is. I used to dream about living there and building a family like you said."

"But you realized it would be hard for you to afford that kind of place."

"It would be impossible. Why do you think I live in an apartment with my brother? It's not just because I love living with Andy, although that's a big part of it."

"I'd want to buy you that house. I'd want to make you happy."

"Buying me a house is even worse than buying me a car."

"Maybe from your point of view, but not from mine. Again, I can afford it. I'll try my best not to be as high-handed as I've been with my money, but I also want to buy things for you. I want for you to relax around money and the thought of not having to count every penny."

"It sounds good, but I know I'm not capable of doing that."

"I think you are. It might take time, but I'm sure we can work together." They wouldn't be mates if they couldn't.

The conversation fizzled out after that. Blair didn't mind, and he could give Jack time to think about what he'd said. He understood better where Jack was coming from now, and he promised himself that he'd be more careful when it came to spending money, no matter how much he wanted to give Jack the world.

"I can head home tonight," Jack said after a moment of silence.

He'd driven from Clifton to Blair's apartment and had left his new car there while Blair drove both of them to the party. Blair at least wanted him to spend the night because they needed to talk more. They'd reached the heart of the problem between them, but they hadn't found a solution yet.

"You can stay the night and go home tomorrow like we discussed," he said. "Or you can head home right now, but if you do, can you call me when you get home?"

Blair could feel Jack's gaze on him. He desperately wanted to ask Jack to stay, but he didn't want to push his mate any more than he already had tonight.

He should have known Jack would be overwhelmed by the party, spending the night, being in the city, and meeting his family. This wasn't the best idea Blair had ever had, and he regretted pushing Jack to come.

"I guess it's late," Jack finally said. "I could stay the night and go home tomorrow after breakfast."

Blair had to work hard not to beam like an idiot. Jack was giving him one more chance, and hopefully, that would be all he needed to convince him they were headed in the right direction when it came to their relationship.

The rest of the ride was silent, which was okay with Blair. He kept thinking about what to say, but he wasn't any closer to finding the magic words that would make everything better by the time they reached his building. Jack kept looking around, and Blair had to admit the city was very different from Clifton, although not in a bad way. Clifton was small and cute and looked like a great place to raise children, much more than the city, if Blair was honest. He had a hard time imagining Jack moving into his apartment, but less so when he thought of himself in a nice little house like the one that belonged to Jack's parents.

Once they got out of the elevator, Blair unlocked his front door and waved Jack inside. Jack was hesitant, but he followed Blair when he moved into the open-space living room. Blair tried to look at his place with Jack's eyes, but he had no idea what Jack expected or was looking for.

He cleared his throat. "You remember where the guest room is?" Although he hoped Jack would sleep in his bed.

Thankfully, Jack seemed to feel the same. Instead of answering Blair, he stepped closer. Blair stayed where he was until Jack's body brushed against his. Then he couldn't resist anymore, and he wrapped his arms around him. Jack tilted his head, but it was Blair who took the last step and finally kissed him.

Kissing Jack was new, yet it felt like coming home. As corny as it sounded, Jack fit perfectly in Blair's arms, and Blair never wanted him to leave. It felt like Jack didn't, either, because he'd grabbed Blair's neck and was clinging to him as if he were afraid that Blair would disappear.

Blair wasn't about to.

Jack's lips were slightly chapped and rough, but Blair didn't mind, because the kiss was soft. Blair was afraid to push Jack in a direction he didn't want, but when Jack leaned back with flushed cheeks and slick lips, he almost lost it.

"Where's the bedroom?" Jack asked in a rough voice.

"The guest room?"

"No. Your bedroom."

Blair hesitated. "We don't have to rush."

"This isn't rushing."

Blair wasn't sure that was the case, but what Jack wanted, Blair would give.

Jack needed to do this. He wanted to be close to Blair for at least one night because he knew it would be their only night.

He'd made his decision, and he hadn't changed his mind even after what Blair had said. There was no way they could compromise, not in a way that wouldn't make one of them unhappy. Blair couldn't leave the city and his fancy apartment and important job, and Jack just wouldn't fit here. He might belong by Blair's side, but not in his life as it was, and he couldn't see a way out of it.

So, he'd leave.

But he wanted to know what Blair felt like just once, to build memories. He didn't know how long it would take him to get over losing Blair or if he'd be able to do that at all, but at least he'd have this.

Thankfully, Blair didn't try to change Jack's mind. He took his hand and pulled him toward the hallway, turning off the light he'd turned on. Darkness folded around them, cradling them and making the situation feel almost unreal. Maybe it was and Jack was dreaming, but if so, he never wanted to wake up.

He pushed that thought away. This would end soon, but he didn't want to think about it yet. He wanted to focus on Blair, and as soon as they stepped into Blair's bedroom, that was what he did.

Jack barely looked at the bedroom long enough to locate the bed. Then he turned to Blair, who was already reaching for his suit jacket. He pushed it off Blair's shoulders, and Blair let him, only helping when Jack looked for a place to set it down. Blair took it from his hand, but instead of being careful about it, he dumped it on the floor and reached for Jack, gently helping him out of his jacket. He then took off both their ties, still as gentle and calm.

From there, Jack knew what to do.

He grabbed Blair's shirt and tried to unbutton it as fast as he could. He felt like whatever was happening would disappear if he wasted time, and he wasn't ready for that.

But Blair obviously knew what to do, even though he couldn't have a clue what was going on in Jack's brain. He wrapped his fingers around Jack's wrist, not to stop him but to slow him down. He squeezed gently, and Jack took a deep breath. He slowed down his fingers, focusing on one button at a time until all of them were undone. Then he pushed the shirt off Blair's shoulders, too, exposing his chest.

Jack's mouth went dry. He'd imagined what Blair looked like naked, but he was still stunned at how gorgeous he was. If he'd had to design the perfect man for him, he'd have made it just like Blair, and the thought was painful. In another life, they could have been great together, but instead, they'd only have this moment.

Blair kissed Jack again, and all thoughts of leaving fled Jack's mind. He focused on the feeling of Blair's lips against his, and he barely realized it when Blair reached for his shirt and unbuttoned it.

Blair's pace forced both of them to move more slowly, and while Jack felt a bit panicky, he also wanted to enjoy this moment. He allowed Blair to set the pace undressing them, and he matched it when he took off Blair's belt, unbuttoned his pants, and slid them down his legs. Next went the shoes and socks, and Blair and Jack were both left wearing only their underwear. Jack knew what to do next, but he still hesitated, because this was Blair. It was his mate. Normally, they'd have the rest of their lives to figure things out and go slow, but they didn't have that time here, even though Blair didn't know it.

But thankfully, Blair seemed to read Jack's mind, at least in part. He knew what Jack needed even though Jack didn't, and it was a relief to let him take over.

He took Jack's hand again and guided him toward the bed, gently pushing him until he fell back onto the mattress.

Jack crawled backward, and Blair followed him. He hooked his fingers under the elastic band of Jack's boxer briefs, and when Jack nodded, pulled them off as gently as he'd done everything else. He was faster with his own underwear, and then they were naked together.

Blair was already hard, and Jack couldn't look away. He didn't know where to start or what he wanted, and like before, he allowed Blair to take over. He wasn't usually so indecisive, but with Blair, he felt he could be. He didn't have to fight to have his voice heard like he did when he was with his brothers. He could be himself, and it was easier when Blair guided him.

So Jack did his best to relax. He let Blair stretch him out on the bed and kiss him. He could feel Blair's hands roam his body, and he loved it. He wished they could have more time, but since he'd have to make do with this, he wanted to make the most of it.

"Lube?" Jack asked.

Blair leaned back. "We have time for that."

They didn't, but Jack couldn't say it. "I need you."

Blair smiled. "And I need you."

This time when he kissed Jack, Jack truly surrendered. He'd do whatever Blair wanted, which apparently was just this. Blair pressed his body on Jack's, and Jack welcomed him, opening his legs and wrapping himself around him.

Usually, Jack was in control in the bedroom, but not this time. Not with Blair.

They moved against each other. Jack felt like he couldn't breathe, and that sensation only diminished when he was touching and kissing Blair, so he did. He licked his way into Blair's mouth, nipped at his lips, and tried to show him how much he meant. Jack had never been good with words—he tended to be too sharp, even when he didn't mean to—but he didn't have to say anything. Blair seemed to understand him, and he made sure they moved without rushing as he mapped Jack's body with his hands.

That was all they did and all they needed. Jack wanted to experience more with Blair, but he also loved just moving against him and feeling his orgasm build. The friction of their stomachs and the hair on Blair's body against his cock drove him nuts, and he snapped his hips upward as he groaned.

Blair seemed to sense that Jack needed more. He raised his hips, but before Jack could complain, he pushed a hand between them. He hooked the other around Jack's shoulders and held him close as he wrapped his hand around their cocks. It was a little dry, but exactly what Jack needed and had been looking for.

Jack moved along with Blair, kissing every inch on his face and neck he could reach and clutching at his shoulders. They panted against each other's mouths, and it felt both like too much and not enough. Then Blair rubbed his thumb on the head of Jack's cock, and pleasure exploded. Blair noticed — of course he did — so he did it again and again as he jacked Jack off. Their cocks rubbed together, and the contrast between the soft skin there and the rougher skin on Blair's hand was everything Jack needed.

He groaned into Blair's mouth and tightened his entire body around his mate. He came between them, and Blair worked his cock through it. Jack felt Blair's whole body tense as he added his release to the slickness between their bodies, and just like Blair had done for him, he held Blair through his peak.

It took them a moment to breathe easier. Jack didn't want to leave, but he knew he'd have to soon. He didn't want Blair to be awake when the time came, which meant they'd have to clean up.

He sat up, and when Blair tried to pull him back down, he shook his head. "Bathroom?"

Blair waved toward a door, and Jack hopped out of bed. He rushed inside, carefully avoided looking at his reflection in the mirror, and wetted a washcloth. He used it to clean himself up, rinsed it, and brought it out to help Blair clean up. He wanted to take care of his mate now while he could do it, and he knew it was the right thing to do when Blair appeared both surprised and pleased at the gesture.

Once they were both clean, they slipped under the blankets, and when Blair reached for Jack, Jack let him. He didn't usually sleep with the guys he had sex with, but Blair wasn't just a guy. Still, it made it harder to resist the pull of sleep, and once Blair was out, to slip out of his arms to leave.

Jack managed without waking Blair, who grunted and hugged the pillow Jack had been resting on as if it were him. Jack's chest tightened at the sight, and he took a moment to look at his mate. It was the last time he could do this, and it made it almost impossible to leave. He was tempted to slide back under the blankets, but instead, he picked up his clothes from the floor and took them to the living room without looking back. He checked that everything he needed was still in his pockets, grabbed his car keys from where he'd left them on the small table by the front door, and put his hand on the door. He took a deep breath, briefly closed his eyes, opened the door, stepped into the hallway, and closed it with a thud that sounded final.

And it was.

CHAPTER SIX

Jack was moping. It was even worse than he'd thought it would be, but he couldn't help it—he missed Blair.

It didn't make sense. They barely knew each other, and he shouldn't miss the guy, even though they were mates. They'd only had one night together, but during that night, Jack felt like he'd opened up his heart and had fallen for Blair. Maybe it was because of the mate bond, or maybe because Blair was just a lovable guy. Whatever the reason, Jack couldn't deny how he felt, and he didn't want to deny it anymore, at least not to himself.

But after listening to Blair talking about how he was ready to change his life for Jack, he'd known he needed to leave. He understood what Blair was saying, but it wasn't fair. Why should Blair change his life so much to be with Jack? Why would he do it when Jack wasn't ready to do the same?

Jack had thought about going back and doing exactly that. He'd tried to imagine himself living in Blair's apartment, going on vacation with his parents to Polynesia, wherever that was, and attending more lavish parties.

He'd been uncomfortable the entire evening, and he knew he would feel the same if he had to attend other parties. He just didn't fit by Blair's side, which was why he'd decided to leave even after they'd talked. Blair had wanted to try to be together, and Jack wanted the same, but he felt like Blair wasn't facing reality.

He could do it for both of them.

Of course, Blair could still find him. He knew where Jack's

parents lived, and he wasn't that far away. He could drive here, try to find Jack, or, as he'd been doing, call and text him. Jack felt guilty about the way he'd left. He should have been honest with Blair and told him to his face that he felt they couldn't work. But instead, he'd fled during the night, abandoning his mate in bed. He hadn't been able to face Blair because his heart had been breaking as it was, and he knew it would have been worse if Blair had been awake. Still, he felt guilty. He'd told Blair they didn't belong together, and Blair hadn't listened. That was all Jack had to say about the reason he left, but he wanted Blair to understand, and he didn't think that was the case. Blair wouldn't have been calling him otherwise.

Blair was perfect where he was, in the city, in that luxurious apartment, with his family in Polynesia. He was made for fundraising parties and expensive cars, but Jack wasn't. Jack was made for his family, the hardware store, and the small apartment he shared with his brother. It wouldn't be fair for either of them to have to change their lives and mold themselves into something they weren't, which meant the only way out of this was the one Jack had taken.

A knock on his bedroom door startled him. He wasn't sure how long he'd been sitting on his bed thinking about Blair, and when he looked at his phone, he grimaced. An hour ago, he'd told his brother he would get ready to go to dinner at their parents' house, but he hadn't even showered.

"Jack?" Andy asked. He sounded worried, which wasn't a surprise.

"I'll be right out," Jack called out.

"You don't have to come if you're not up for it. You know Mom and Dad won't say anything about it."

Maybe not to his face, but Jack knew his family was worried. They'd been walking on eggshells around him since he'd come back from the party, and no one had dared ask him what had happened with Blair. It was like they were afraid he'd explode if they did, and while he wouldn't, he was relieved he didn't have to explain himself to anyone.

He already knew what his parents and his brothers would say. They'd tell him he was an idiot and that Blair was his mate, which meant they were destined to be together. They'd tell him to try again, to make more of an effort, and maybe he would. Maybe he'd decide he should move in with Blair after all, and he'd go, and Blair would forgive him for what he'd done.

And then, maybe next week, in a month, or next year, Jack would realize how much of a mistake he'd made. He never wanted to come to resent Blair, which was one of the reasons he had every intention of staying in Clifton.

He hauled himself up and went to open the door. "I'm coming," he said, not looking at his brother.

"We can go whenever you want. I'm ready."

Jack looked down. He was still wearing the same clothes he'd worn at work, which, thankfully, weren't dirty, but he still sniffed his armpits just in case. He wasn't shower-fresh, but he'd do, and before following Andy to the front door, he quickly sprayed deodorant under his t-shirt. He forced a smile on his face, even though he knew Andy wouldn't fall for it, and followed his brother out the door.

Thankfully, Andy didn't ask questions. He'd been tiptoeing around Jack like the rest of their family, but Jack had expected at least him to say something considering how close they were. He seemed to understand that Jack had nothing to say about what happened, though. Eventually, they'd talk, but the pain was too fresh in Jack's heart for him to want to do so now.

"Okay, I've had enough," Andy said eventually.

Jack groaned and pressed his forehead against the window. "Can we not right now?"

"Do you want to wait until we reach Mom and Dad's house and our entire family stages an intervention?"

Jack glared. "That's what you've been plotting?"

"Do you really think we'd let you continue whatever you've been doing? We have eyes, and we can see you're not yourself. Something happened when you were in the city with Blair, and we waited for you to talk to us, but you haven't."

"It's only been a few days," Jack complained.

"It's been two weeks. And I know Blair has tried contacting you. Hell, he's even called me, but I had nothing to tell him because I didn't know what to say."

Jack wasn't surprised Blair had called his brother. "When did he get your phone number?"

"When you told him to fuck off because he'd bought you a car. I promised I'd make sure you'd accept it, but I also told him he had to talk to you. Is that what happened when you were in the city? Did the two of you talk?"

Flashes of that night made Jack close his eyes. He didn't want to think about what had happened between him and Blair. It hurt too much. "We talked," he confirmed. There was no way to avoid this, especially not when his family was involved. They wouldn't let this go, no matter how much he wished they would.

"And you decided you couldn't be together?"

"We *can't* be together, Andy. There's no way it could work, and it's better for us to be hurt now than in a year or two."

"You decided that on your own, didn't you?"

"What do you think? Blair doesn't see it, but I do. I don't fit in his life, and he doesn't fit in mine, so it wouldn't be fair for either of us to have to leave everything behind for the other. I don't want to come to resent him, and I don't want him to resent me, either."

"You're sure you can't fit in his life then."

"You should have seen it. His apartment is incredible, and that party. It was like nothing I've ever seen."

"And you don't want to leave Clifton."

"My entire life is here. There's you, the family, the store." And the house Jack still walked past every day if he could.

The owners had put it up for sale last week, and Jack had been stunned. He'd even gone over his finances in the hope he might be able to buy it, even though he'd known he couldn't. That hurt almost as much as losing Blair, especially when he learned later that the house had been sold. Now it was out of his life, just like his mate.

"I'm fine," he said. "And I don't want to talk about this anymore."

"Fine, but don't think this is over."

Jack had no doubt it wasn't. He knew his family and how they worked. He wasn't sure he'd be ready to stand whatever conversation was about to happen, but at least he had a few minutes to shield himself.

Whatever good it would do.

We're here.

Blair stared at his phone's screen for a moment before taking a deep breath and putting it on the counter. He looked around one last time, but there wasn't anything to see. The house was empty, but hopefully, that wouldn't last long.

It all depended on whether or not Jack forgave him for buying it for him.

Blair had promised he wouldn't buy anything big for Jack without consulting him first, and he'd had every intention of keeping that promise until Jack had disappeared into the night. Blair had only been half surprised to wake up on his own the morning after the party, but he'd hoped against all hope he'd find Jack in his kitchen, maybe getting breakfast ready. The apartment had been empty, and so had Blair's life since then. No matter how many times he called Jack or how many times he texted him, Jack never answered.

So Blair had called Andy.

He didn't know what he would have done if Jack's brother hadn't gone along with this. Blair wanted to be with Jack, and he'd had a vague idea of how to make that happen, but he'd only been able to figure out parts of the plan on his own. For the rest, he'd needed someone in Clifton, and Andy had been the best partner in crime Blair could have hoped for.

He'd been the one who told Blair that the house Jack had dreamed about since he was a kid was for sale. Blair had snatched it up before anyone else could. And once again, Andy had been the one to tell him how disappointed Jack had been when he'd realized he couldn't buy it, then again when he'd seen it had been sold. Blair hoped that Jack's love for the house would help him accept that Blair had bought it. And in turn, the gesture would show Jack how much he meant to Blair and that Blair wanted him in his life, even if they had to make compromises.

And Blair was ready to make most of them.

He understood why Jack didn't want to leave Clifton and why Jack felt out of place at the party and with his family. He couldn't deny that was the case, although he hoped Jack would give his parents and his sister a chance. They didn't care what Jack did for a living. They just wanted Blair to be happy, and even though they were disappointed that Blair was moving away, they understood why he was doing so. They didn't want him to lose his mate, and his father had been more than happy to agree to let Blair work from home and commute to the city only a couple times a week. It wouldn't be fun, but Blair was ready to do this and so much more for Jack, and besides, there was nothing that said things had to continue this way for years. They could reassess in a year or two and see what happened then.

First, Blair had to convince Jack to give him a second chance.

He grabbed his wallet, keys, and phone from the table and pushed them into his jeans pockets. He made sure to lock the door, even though there was nothing in the house to steal. He looked around, wanting the house to make a good impression when Jack first saw it, but there was nothing he could do. He was lucky he'd managed to convince the old owners to give him the keys only two weeks after they'd sold the house to him. He supposed that no matter how little Jack liked that he had money, sometimes it came in handy.

Blair didn't take his car. The house was only a few blocks away from the one where Jack's parents lived, so Blair would walk there. Hopefully, he wouldn't have to do the walk of shame back to the house after Jack rejected him.

Blair had made a lot of big decisions without Jack's input, and he was afraid Jack would freak out because he hadn't been involved. The thing was that Blair had tried to involve him. As soon as he'd realized that Jack was gone the day after the party, he'd called him. When it had been clear that Jack wouldn't answer his phone, Blair had known he'd have to take things into his own hands. He couldn't talk to Jack about moving to Clifton and finding a home for the two of them, and that was truly Jack's fault, just like it was Jack's fault that they hadn't talked before the party. Jack tended to retreat when he was angry or sad, and this situation wasn't any different. He'd retreated into his shell, and from what Andy had said, he wasn't letting anyone in, not even his family. He was in pain, and Blair hoped that showing him he didn't have to be would help.

He wasn't sure what he'd do otherwise.

He was nervous as he reached the house where Jack was. His eyes widened when he saw how many cars were parked in the driveway and in front of the house, and he knew Andy had talked to his family. From the number of cars, Blair was pretty sure every single brother was there, probably with their mates. That meant he'd have a public fight, and while he wasn't exactly happy about it, he understood this was how things would go from now on. Jack's family was important to him, possibly the most important thing in the world, and they'd always be involved in the decisions he and Blair would make together, even though they were a couple.

It was odd, but Blair couldn't say he minded. Still, he hoped they weren't about to see him get his ass handed to him by Jack.

He stopped in front of the house and took out his phone. He quickly texted Andy, then he waited.

It only took a few moments for Andy to appear at the front door. He quietly closed it behind himself, and Blair strode toward him. They hadn't seen each other since that time Andy had promised Jack would take the car Blair had bought him, but they'd talked almost every day since Jack had returned to Clifton, and Blair felt as if he knew Andy now.

"He's bitchy," Andy said as a hello.

Blair found himself smiling. "When isn't he?"

"I suppose you're not wrong. I just wanted you to know what you're about to walk into."

Blair grimaced. "You're still sure this is the best way to do this?"

"Well, you didn't like the idea of locking the two of you in the closet."

"You could have locked us in his bedroom."

Andy shook his head. "That wouldn't have worked. Jack needs his bedroom to be the one place where he knows he's safe. He would have freaked out if you'd tried talking to him there. This house, on the other hand, is neutral. He doesn't live here, and neither do you. Neither of you comes here when you need help or just to be comforted."

"I find it hard to believe," Blair murmured. Surely, Jack liked to be comforted by his parents?

Or maybe not. From what Blair knew about Jack, he didn't let anyone see he needed comfort. He held his shield up high, hid behind his mask, and acted as if everything in his world was all right, even when it was clear that wasn't the case.

"Have you changed your mind?" Andy asked, his tone harsher.

"Of course not. Jack is my mate, and I want him in my life. I wouldn't have moved otherwise. I wouldn't have bought him a house."

Andy snickered. "About that, I wish I could record the moment you'll tell him. He's going to be pissed."

And that was what worried Blair. "Even though it's his dream house?"

"That's probably the only reason he won't kill you. You should have seen how sad he was when he found out it'd been sold. He really wanted that house."

"And now, it's his." Because Blair had put both their names on the documents. Jack would need to sign them, but the only thing that mattered was that the house was theirs and that hopefully, they'd build a future and a family together there.

Andy patted Blair's shoulder. "He's going to be pissed. You know him, and you know that he uses his anger as a shield. Don't let him get to you. He wants to be with you as much as you want to be with him, even though he's been trying to hide it, even from himself. He's been moping since he came back. No matter how much he screams and yells at you, deep inside, he wants the same thing you do."

Happiness. That was all Blair wanted, both for himself and Jack, and he hoped he was about to get it.

Jack frowned when Andy came back in. "You were outside

for a while," he said.

Andy shrugged. "I had to talk to someone."

That didn't reassure Jack. "Is everything okay? Can I help you with anything?" He hoped his brother wasn't in trouble. Jack would help him if he was, but his mind wasn't in it.

He felt like it was stuck on Blair since he'd met his mate, and he didn't know how to deal with it. No matter how many times he told himself to stop thinking about the man and focus on his family and what he had here in Clifton, his thoughts returned to his mate on their own. There was no way for Jack to stop thinking about him, and it was especially hard when his family tried to convince him to give Blair another chance.

That was why everyone was here tonight. Jack hadn't been surprised to see all the cars lining the street. Andy had said everyone was worried about Jack, so the intervention made sense. Jack wished he could have gone without it, but this was his family. They wouldn't allow him to wallow in his pain and unhappiness if there was anything they could do about it, and they'd be sure there *was* something they could do about it until Jack convinced them otherwise.

Nothing could solve his problem. Nothing could heal his heart. He'd been the one to break it, and while some days he regretted it, he also felt it was for the best for everyone.

Or at least, that was what he kept telling himself.

A knock on the door made Jack blink. He looked around, sure one of his brothers or their mates would get up and open it, but instead, they were all staring at him. It was honestly a bit creepy, and he didn't understand what was going on.

"What?" he asked.

"Can you please open the door?" Jack's mother asked.

He looked at her where she was sitting on the arm of his father's favorite armchair. Jack's father had his arm around her waist, holding her close. It was strange to see her there instead of in the kitchen cooking, but she'd prepared lasagna, and she'd said there was nothing else to do but for her to wait for it to be ready.

"Shouldn't *you* be the one to open it?" Jack asked.

"I'm having a conversation with Manuel."

"Then someone else can open it." There were so many of them that not everyone could be busy.

But as Jack looked around, everyone made a show of not looking at him and getting busy. Hugh and Sean had their heads close together, seemingly talking about a new job Sean had just agreed to take on. Curtis, Richie, Peter, and Gilbert were watching something on Richie's phone and carefully not looking at Jack. Laurie, Alexis, Leon, and Melissa were playing on the floor.

Andy was still there, doing nothing, but when Jack opened his mouth to tell him he should open it since he'd just been outside, he shook his head. "Get off your ass and open the door," he said.

Jack grunted and got to his feet. "When has everyone gotten so lazy?" he whined.

"We could say the same about you. Why don't you want to open the door?"

Jack hauled himself to his feet. "I'm going. I'm going. But I'll remember this."

For some reason, Andy snickered. "I bet you will," he muttered as Jack passed by him.

Jack ignored him. All his brothers were strange in their own way, and Andy wasn't any different.

Jack stomped his way to the front door and threw it open, ready to tell whoever it was to fuck off. His thoughts froze when he saw Blair standing on his parents' doorstep.

It was the first time they'd seen each other in two weeks, and Blair looked fucking good. The sight of him there, wearing jeans and a t-shirt, was odd, but it made Jack want to throw himself into his mate's arms. He almost did, too, until he remembered that he and Blair weren't together.

He swallowed, but his mouth had gone dry, and it didn't help. "What are you doing here?" he asked. His tone was too harsh, but Blair didn't seem to mind.

"I came to talk to you."

Blair sounded soft and gentle, and Jack felt he didn't deserve it. He didn't deserve many things, and one of them was Blair.

Jack started to shake his head, but something hit him on the back and pushed him forward. He stumbled out of the house, twisting to see what was happening. Blair caught him and pulled him close, and at the same time, Andy slammed the front door shut and locked it.

He'd pushed Jack into Blair's arms, quite literally.

Jack straightened and shook off Blair's hands. He scowled at the door, because he was sure his brother was spying on him from the small window there. "You do realize there's a back door, right?" he asked.

"We locked that one, too," Andy said.

Of course they had. "You planned all of this, didn't you?"

The curtain at the small window moved, and his brother's face appeared. "We did. Now stop being an asshole and talk to your mate. He has something to tell you."

Jack sucked in a breath. He wanted to talk to Blair. Hell, he wanted to do so much more than talk to him. He wanted to throw himself into Blair's arms and never let go. He wanted to apologize, say he'd been an idiot, and beg Blair to give him another chance.

Was that why Blair was here? What other reason would he have to want to see Jack and rope Jack's family into planning all of this?

Jack slowly turned to face his mate. Now that he took a better look, he could see that Blair was tired. He still looked good, but he was a little pale, and the shadows under his eyes were darker than they'd been the last time they'd seen each other.

"Haven't you been sleeping?" he asked.

Once again, Blair didn't seem to mind his tone. "I've had a few difficulties sleeping," Blair admitted. "You know how it is. I keep wondering why my mate abandoned me. It hasn't been easy to let go of those thoughts to get some sleep."

Jack grunted. "You have to take care of yourself."

"What do you care? You left me."

And Blair was clearly angry about that. "Are you here to yell at me because of that? Because if that's the case, have at me." Jack didn't care if it meant he could spend a little more time with Blair.

Blair's eyes narrowed. "Andy was right."

"My brother is never right. What did he say?"

"That you haven't been yourself. Why? Why did you leave me when we were trying to work things out?"

"I left because it was the only thing that made sense. It wouldn't be fair to ask you to move here, just like it wouldn't be fair for me to move to the city. We'd both come to resent the other, and our relationship would break."

"So you decided to stop that before we could have a chance?"

"It was better that way. I know we're both hurting over this, but it would have been much worse if we waited a year or two. You might not see things the way I do, but we can't work together." Jack wished they could, though.

"I bought your house."

Jack stared. He couldn't have heard that right. "I'm sorry?"

"You heard me. I bought your house. Actually, I bought *you* your dream house. You know, the one you told me about. Andy let me know it was up for sale, and I bought it before anyone else could."

Jack could only continue staring. He heard the words and

understood their meaning, but his brain was frozen for some reason. The only thing he could focus on was that Blair had just said he'd bought him his dream house, and Jack had no idea what it meant.

That seemed to give Blair the push he needed to explain. He straightened his back and held Jack's gaze as he continued, "And I've started the process of moving here. I already talked to my father and my sister, and they agree it's the best thing for you and me. I'll work from home most of the time and commute a couple times a week to the city. My sister is taking on the everyday tasks, so it won't be a problem."

Jack still couldn't make his lips move. Blair had just made his brain explode, or at least, that was what it felt like.

Had Blair really moved to Clifton? And he'd bought Jack a house?

He was doing this for Jack, to be with him, and Jack had to do or say something, but he continued staring.

Blair had known Jack would be angry, but he hadn't expected the stillness. It was as if Jack's brain couldn't wrap around what Blair had just told him, which made sense, since it was huge. Still, Blair was getting worried. He needed Jack to react, even if it was to yell at him.

"Jack?" he said softly. He reached for Jack and touched his mate's arm.

That seemed to get Jack into motion again. He jerked away, which hurt, but Blair tried not to let it get to him. Jack was overwhelmed, and if he needed space, he should take it.

Jack wrapped his arms around himself. It was an odd gesture of fragility Blair had never seen on his mate and hadn't expected. He wanted to pull Jack into his arms and tell him everything would be okay, but first, he needed to know what Jack was thinking.

By buying the house and moving, Blair had taken a chance. What if Jack didn't like him and didn't want him as a mate? What if Jack's problem with them being mates wasn't the distance, and he'd just been using that as an excuse? What if he didn't want Blair and couldn't love him?

But no. Jack had shown Blair how much he meant through his gestures when they'd been together after the party. He'd been as eager as Blair to get into bed, and while Blair had been in control, Jack had taken care of him afterward. He wouldn't have if he didn't want Blair.

"Why did you move?" Jack finally asked.

"Because you didn't want to move to the city."

Jack shook his head. "But it doesn't make sense. Your job is there. Your family is there. Don't you want to be with them?"

"I'm close to my family, but nowhere near as close as you are to yours. I see my father and my sister every day at work, but I only see my mother about once a week, and the same goes for my brother-in-law and niece and nephew. Sometimes it goes even longer than that because one of us is on a trip. Besides, it's only a one-hour drive. If I want to see my sister, I can get in the car and drive. But you see your parents and your brothers every day. You spend time with them, and I know how important that is to you. I couldn't take that away, especially when I knew you didn't want to lose all of this. So, I moved."

Jack shook his head. "But why?"

"Because I won't give you up. If you can't leave Clifton, then I'll come to you. If this is the only place where you can be happy, I'll follow you. Nothing is more important than you. Not my family, not my job, not my apartment. The only thing I see in my future is you, and I hope the same goes for you and that you can accept that just like you've made your decision that you can't move, I've decided that I could, and I did. *You're* my home Jack, wherever you are."

Jack licked his lips. He was still staring, but Blair thought he could see signs of softening.

"Won't you have to go to work every day?" Jack asked.

"Most of my days are focused on phone calls and emails. If there's a meeting I can't avoid sitting in on, I'll drive there. Otherwise, my father or my sister can take care of it. Stop trying to find flaws in my plan. I've thought about everything, and I know my job and what I need to do for it better than you. If I tell you I can work from home and commute a couple times a week, then I can, and I will. And when I come home, I'll be coming home to you."

Jack rubbed his face. He looked like he was about to break down, but Blair couldn't tell if that was a good thing. He didn't want to hurt his mate, but he did want to get to the center of Jack, behind the shield and the mask. Jack used his anger so that no one could see the real him, but Blair wanted to be the one person who would.

"What if I'm not enough?" Jack asked.

"How could you not be?" Blair remembered what Jack had said about not fitting in and not being good enough. He wasn't sure how he could change Jack's mind about that, but even if it took him years, he'd do it. "You're my mate. But more importantly, you're *you*. You might not have lived the same life I have, and you might not be used to the same things, but it doesn't mean you're not good enough. You're just different, and being in a relationship means finding compromises to be together. I'm moving here, and maybe, sometimes, you could come to some of the fundraising parties and events for my work. I'll keep the apartment in case I need a home base in the city, so we can spend the night there and come home the next day, or not. Whatever you want. I just want us to try to mesh our lives together, because I'm convinced it can work if we give us a chance."

"What if it doesn't work?" Jack asked.

Blair felt they'd finally reached the heart of the problem. "What if it does?"

Jack glared at him. "Stop that. I'm serious."

"If it doesn't work, well, we'll have tried. Do you really want to regret not attempting this? Wouldn't it be better to have tried even if it fails?"

"That's easy to say when you wouldn't be the one at fault."

Blair wasn't entirely sure why Jack felt that way. He understood how different they and their lives were, but why did that have to mean that Jack wasn't good enough? "Why wouldn't it be? Maybe I'll do something that you won't be able to forgive. Why do you assume that if our relationship fails, it will be your fault?"

Jack shrugged and looked away. "You're kind of the perfect guy, aren't you? You're handsome, elegant, have a great job, earn a lot of money, all that stuff."

"That doesn't make me perfect. It makes me *me*, and I'm quite happy with the person I am."

The corner of Jack's lips curled. "I'm quite happy with the person you are, too."

"There's no way to know if our relationship will work, or if it doesn't, whose fault it will be. We can obsess over that and try to fix things before they happen, or we can focus on each other, build a relationship, and be happy. I know which one I'd rather do, but what about you?"

Blair held his breath as he waited for Jack to answer. He had no idea what his mate would say, but he hoped Jack would finally see beyond his shield. It didn't matter if Jack wasn't the perfect guy. Blair didn't need him to be perfect. He just needed him to give their relationship a chance, and he was sure that everything else would come in time.

They were mates for a reason, and Blair prayed that Jack would see that.

Jack squinted. "You bought me a house."

Blair wondered what that had to do with the conversation. "I did. It's your dream house."

"How did you know?"

"Your brother. We've been talking since you left, and he told me the house was up for sale."

"He planned all of this, didn't he?"

Blair took a chance and reached for Jack. When Jack didn't move away, Blair linked their fingers together, pulling him closer. "Your brother loves you, and he wants you to be happy, like the rest of your family." Like Blair.

"And he thinks I'll be happy with you?"

"Why wouldn't you be? I have every intention of making you as happy as humanly possible for the rest of our lives."

"That sounds complicated."

Blair had no doubt it would be, knowing Jack. Still, he was up for the challenge. "Will you give me a chance to try?"

Finally, Jack smiled. It illuminated his face, and he stepped closer, wrapping his arms around him. "I will," Jack said. He grinned at Blair. "But first, we have to talk about you buying me expensive stuff like a *house*."

Blair laughed. He didn't care if Jack yelled at him for buying the house. As long as Jack was in his life and his arms, he'd take whatever Jack threw at him.

Chapter Seven

The house was coming along nicely, and Jack couldn't help but feel satisfied as he looked around the kitchen.

He'd been tempted to yell at Blair for buying the house, but he hadn't been able to. Not only had Blair done everything he could to get Jack to accept him in his life, but he'd also made his dreams come true.

Jack had the house of his dreams. It was his, and he found himself smiling every time he thought about it. His heart was so full that it felt like it was about to burst, but Jack hoped it wouldn't, because he had things to do.

And he was nervous.

"I already told you not to worry about my family," Blair said. He kissed Jack's neck, making Jack shudder.

Jack plastered a glare on his face. It was getting harder and harder to scowl at everyone these days. Jack was too happy. "How am I not supposed to worry about them? I didn't make the best first impression when I met your parents, and I've never talked to your sister."

"My parents like you, and my sister will love you. You just have to give them a chance."

And to do so, Jack would have to be open.

Some days, he still wasn't sure this was the best thing he and Blair could do, but to his surprise, they made it work. Blair had insisted on renovating the house, and most of it was done by now. The guest bedrooms were the only things left to do, but it wasn't urgent.

Sometimes, Jack wondered if they truly needed such a big

house. There were four bedrooms and only two of them. They shared the master bedroom, of course. And when Jack had pointed out they didn't need so much space, Blair had shut him up with a kiss and by telling him it was for his family. This way, they could spend the night when they came over.

Neither of them had said it, but Jack hoped it would be enough space for their children one day. It wasn't something they'd talked about, but they would, and soon. First, though, Jack wanted to get over the hurdle of meeting Blair's family again.

Several months had passed since the party, and they didn't make Jack any less nervous. Jack's parents loved Blair, and Jack prayed that Blair's parents would love him, but it was hard to believe. Jack knew how he was—abrasive, always with a scowl on his face, and some people would say, bitchy.

But living with Blair and being with him had softened Jack. He couldn't deny it, even though he didn't like it.

Well, maybe that wasn't the entire truth. He didn't have a reason to be rough anymore. He had everything he'd ever wanted and had never allowed himself to get. He was still working at the hardware store, and Mr. Thomas was making noises about retiring next year, or maybe the one after that. Jack had the house of his dream, and it was even more gorgeous than how he'd imagined it would be.

And of course, he had his mate.

Sometimes, Jack was still hesitant, but Blair was a dream come true just as much as the house. He had what seemed like endless patience when it came to Jack's prickliness, and he didn't hesitate to show his affection. He never demanded things from Jack that Jack wasn't ready to give, and he'd taken to living in Clifton like a duck to water.

Most weekends, the two of them shifted and flew around town. Jack had only ever done that with his brothers and his parents, and they still had to be careful, because people would notice an Osprey and a swan flying around, but he loved it. It gave them an opportunity to be together without talking about feelings and whatever else worried Jack.

And Jack was worried. He supposed he would always be. No matter how many times Blair told him he was perfect the way he was and that he liked living in Clifton, Jack couldn't help the doubts that rose during the moments in which he didn't have anything else to do or think about. He supposed only time would help him feel better about it. And for once, that didn't scare him, because he and Blair *had* time.

Blair kissed Jack's cheek and stepped away. "Come on. Your family is going to start to arrive, and Lisa texted me that they're almost here, too."

Jack swallowed and looked around one last time. One of the reasons he loved his house so much was the large back yard. Blair had had a new deck installed, and they were having both their families over for dinner. They'd eat outside under the stars, and since Jack had been freaking out about the house not being perfect, Blair had hired a decorator. There were flowers seemingly everywhere, candles ready to be lit, and lamps that bathed the deck in a warm glow. The food was being catered, so Jack didn't even have to think about that, which was good, yet at the same time, a problem because it gave him too much time to think about everything else.

The sound of the doorbell made him jump. He looked at Blair, panic rising in his chest, but Blair's presence was a rock. Blair kissed Jack's forehead, took his hand, and pulled him toward the front door.

"Everything is perfect," he said. "The food is already in the oven waiting to be warmed, and the bottles of wine and champagne are in the fridge. The only thing you have to worry about is having fun."

"A dinner with my family is more like torture," Jack muttered as Blair opened the door.

Jack's mother was the first to walk in. She opened her arms to hug Blair, and Blair easily went. "Happy birthday," she said.

The party was both for Blair's birthday and to show off their new home. Jack was glad they'd only have to do this once, and he was relieved Blair had thought about it and didn't mind.

"Thank you, and welcome," Blair answered.

Jack's family seemed to have decided to arrive together because they filed in after Jack's mother. Blair shook hands and hugged whoever wanted to be hugged, while Jack glared at every single member of his family. He was glad to see them and spend the evening with them, but he couldn't show them how happy he was. He had a reputation to maintain, after all.

They didn't even have time to close the door when Blair's parents appeared on the doorstep. Jack swallowed and plastered a smile on his face, praying everything would be okay and that Blair wouldn't regret giving Jack a chance.

To his surprise, Blair's mother hugged him. "It's such a pleasure to see you again."

"I apologize I didn't visit you sooner," Jack said, his voice tense.

"Oh, don't worry about it. We understood when Blair told us about the house and his move. We weren't surprised you wanted to spend time together and get settled." She stepped away and looked around. "And it's absolutely gorgeous."

Jack found himself puffing out his chest. "Thank you."

The renovations had only been possible thanks to Blair's money. Jack still had trouble accepting how much wealthier Blair was, but it was getting easier now that he saw how Blair intended to spend his money.

In the beginning, it had been hard to accept that Blair had bought them a house and didn't expect Jack to repay him, but Blair had pointed out that hopefully, they'd both live here for the rest of their lives, and they'd raise a family. Wasn't that better than renting an apartment so they could split costs? Jack hadn't been able to say that Blair was wrong, and he'd agreed to let his mate pay for the renovations and most of the bills. They'd hired Sean, so everything had stayed in the family, which had helped soothe Jack's fears that he was taking advantage of Blair.

It would take time and possibly more people pushing him, since he was as stubborn as a mule, but he'd wrap his mind around all of this, and he'd eventually come to accept that he *was* what Blair wanted and that his mate wasn't leaving him. They were building a life together, and like Blair had said, it would be for the rest of their lives.

Jack couldn't wait.

ABOUT THE AUTHOR

Catherine is the creator of several series, most of them paranormal, including the Whitedell Pride Series and the Gillham Pack Series. While she graduated in translation, she decided to go the writer's way because it was more fun to create her own stories and characters.

She's been living in Italy for more than twenty years, but she's a daughter of the North—Belgium to be precise—and she misses it so much that she's already planning to move back.

She loves pizza—probably too much—her son, her pets, and of course, books. She sneaks some reading time into her schedule every time she has five minutes free from writing, demands from her various pets and son, and lastly, housework.

Connect with her:

lievens.catherine@gmail.com
BookBub: https://www.bookbub.com/authors/catherine-lievens
Website: https://authorcatherinelievens.com/
Facebook: https://www.facebook.com/catherine.lievens.9
Facebook Group: https://www.facebook.com/groups/411788002341528/
Twitter: https://twitter.com/authorCLievens
Newsletter: http://eepurl.com/c-uvKn

www.ingramcontent.com/pod-product-compliance
Lightning Source LLC
Chambersburg PA
CBHW060632130626
46555CB00002B/771